A Cold and Calculating Tail
A Sassy Sarcastic Cat Cozy Mystery

Rachel Woods

BONZAI
MOON

BONZAI
MOON

BonzaiMoon Books LLC
Houston, Texas
www.bonzaimoonbooks.com

Hey, y'all, hey!!!

Subscribe to my newsletter and you'll get inspiring rescue stories, hilarious cat memes, and thrilling serialized fiction. Plus, you can find out first about new books featuring my fabulous life as a feisty, fierce feline, and much more!

Sign me up!

Sassy Callie

https://subscribepage.io/SassyCallie

Prologue

Since the unfortunate incident, which occurred a month ago, whereupon I was viciously and savagely attacked by Callie, the homeless Calico cat—who may or may not be homeless but who is absolutely a Calico cat with the distinctive orange and black patches —my life has changed tremendously.

How, you might ask?

Well, for one, I've become a better investigative reporter. Not the world's best. Not yet. I am, however, actively striving toward the completion of that goal, you'll be thrilled to know.

And, for two, Callie the (somewhat) homeless Calico cat talks to me.

Yes, you read that right.

The cat talks.

And I understand every word she says. All her meows and purrs and trills and growls and yowls and hisses sound like perfect English.

How, you might ask?

Well, I'm not quite sure.

Since the cat started speaking to me, I have spent some time trying to figure out how I can communicate with the feline. I haven't come to a definitive conclusion. When Callie attacked me, she bit me pretty severely. I still have a reminder of her savagery. A scar between my thumb and forefinger where she sank her teeth into my flesh, leaving me bleeding and feverish.

As it turned out, the wound became infected. I went to the hospital and got antibiotics, which were supposed to clear the bacteria from my bloodstream. Instead, in a bizarre and cruel twist of fate, the medicine caused an allergic reaction that was so drastic, I ended up in a coma for three days!

Ironically, I was in the hospital when Callie first spoke to me.

But, truthfully, I'm not totally convinced that the cat and I are talking to each other.

I mean, I think we are ...

And, sometimes, I think I'm suffering the effects of the trauma from her attack. Maybe I'm suffering from PTSD. Or perhaps my belief that I can talk to Callie is nothing more than a strange manifestation of my subconscious. Maybe it's all in my head. Maybe I'm dreaming. Or—

Or maybe the Calico and I really speak to each other.

I don't mean to be wishy-washy but I'm in a strange, extraordinary situation, one that's super hard to wrap my head around, and I'm still adjusting. On the one hand, a talking cat is pretty cool. But, on the other, it's also disturbingly weird.

Anyway, for now, I'm just going to accept that Callie and I can communicate, which is rather helpful since the Calico is committed to helping me get my *Palmchat Gazette* byline changed. With her assistance, I'll go from Sophie Carter, Junior Reporter to Sophie Carter, Senior Investigative Reporter in no time.

Maybe.

Hopefully.

I think ...

Chapter 1

At eight in the morning on a gloomy, overcast Tuesday, I'm not doing what I would normally be doing, which is drinking dragon fruit and pear tea, eating donut holes drizzled with a brown sugar glaze, and checking my social media feeds.

Now, technically, and perhaps logically, what I *should* be doing is fact-checking my latest articles and making phone calls to witnesses who could provide more details for said articles, but that's not what I'm doing.

Unfortunately, at the moment, I am hypercritically and unabashedly being chewed out by my boss, Martin "Marty" Edwards, the Editor of the *Palmchat Gazette* St. Mateo satellite office, where I'm currently employed as a Junior Reporter.

"In addition to the fact that you didn't provide enough details in the stories I assigned to you," bellows Marty, whose face grows more florid with each second as he paces back and forth behind his desk, smashing a stress ball between his palms. "You also went out of your way to do feature stories that I never asked for!"

I bite my bottom lip and then try to explain. "Well, yes, that's true, but—"

Marty scowls at me. "Did I ask you to write an article about a woman who believes chocolate milk is being used to control the minds of first graders?"

"Second graders," I correct.

Marty frowns. "What?"

"Only second graders are being subjected to mind control."

Folding his arms, Marty asks, "And you know this how?"

"Because the lunch lady told me," I say. "After all she's in a unique position to know."

"And what unique position is that?"

"She works in the school cafeteria and personally hands out chocolate milk to every second grader at the school."

"But what proof does she have that the chocolate milk is being used in mind control?" asks Marty.

"Proof?" I echo.

"You didn't even bother to find out, did you?" Marty shakes his head.

"Well …"

"And then there was the story about the man who believes he was abducted by rabid bats he encountered while exploring a cave."

"That was one of my more popular stories," I say, figuring I might as well toot my own horn.

"Yes, it was," agrees Marty. "But you left out crucial details."

Again, I try to explain. "Well, yes, that's true, but—"

"You didn't inform the readers that the bats in question were not, in fact, rabid."

"I didn't?" I ask, trying to remember if I recall that detail.

"You didn't," confirms Marty.

"Are you sure?"

Marty looks like a cranky, boiled lobster as he scowls at me. "Trust me, you didn't. And you also didn't tell the readers that the man who told you about said bats was a psycho who had escaped from the Rakestraw-Blake Center's Neuropsychology Facility."

"A psycho?" My mouth drops open. "Are you serious?"

Marty scowls. "I'm always serious."

Staring at him, I beg to differ. He can't always be serious, can he? I mean, there have to be some moments when he's flippant, trivial, and irreverent, right?

Clearing my throat, I say, "Well, I only asked because he didn't seem particularly psychotic."

"Particularly psychotic?"

"He wasn't ranting and raving, or drooling, or thrashing about, or trapped in the throes of an apoplectic fit, or—"

"Be that as it may," Marty goes on, "I was informed by the St. Mateo police chief that the department was inundated with people terrified of being bitten by rabid bats when they should have been afraid of the man since after your interview, he subsequently attacked three people."

"Yes, well, that is very unfortunate, but—"

"You caused unnecessary panic and the cave exploration tourism sector took a blow."

"Yes, well, again, that is very unfortunate, but—"

"And let's not forget the story about the man who got up in the middle of the night for a mini-Snickers bar but instead accidentally picked up a cockroach, swallowed it, and nearly choked to death—"

"Almond Joy," I correct.

Martin scowls. "What?"

"It wasn't a mini-Snickers," I say. "It was a mini–Almond Joy."

"You do understand that it doesn't matter what kind of mini chocolate bar the man nearly choked on, don't you?"

"Actually, it does matter," I dispute, which I probably shouldn't since Marty's face is turning even redder, which I didn't think was even remotely possible. Nevertheless, I feel I should forge on, and press ahead. "We have to get the facts right, right? We can't accuse Snickers of something Almond Joy did, can we?"

Marty stares at me.

I clear my throat.

Sighing, Marty drops down into his leather chair. "Listen, Sophia, I will—grudgingly and somewhat against my will and better judgment—admit that the stories were interesting—"

"They were?" I ask.

"And they trended—"

"They did?"

"And got decent engagement."

"Are you serious?"

"But …" Marty gives me a stern expression as he holds up a hand. "The writing still was not the best and there were a lot of details you didn't provide."

Slightly deflated, I nod. "That's true."

"For those reasons and so many others, too many to name, we'd be here all day and all night, you are still on probation."

Completely deflated, I sigh.

"But you are getting …"

"Better?" I ask, hopeful.

Marty shakes his head as he gives me one of those sardonic smiles that lack any warmth or mirth. "I wouldn't go that far."

"How far would you go?" I ask.

Pressing the heel of his palm against his blotchy red forehead, Marty says, "If you want to go far, Sophia, in your career here at the *Palmchat Gazette*—"

"I want to go as far as possible," I say.

"Then I need more details in your stories," says Marty, pointing a warning finger at me. "And you can start with that story you did last week about that diamond heist. It needs more details. You need to talk to the police. Find out the status of the investigation."

"I actually did talk to the police," I tell Marty. "But they didn't want to comment."

"The cops never want to comment," says Marty. "You can't let them ignore you. Did you talk to your police source?"

My police source is Officer Noah Cuetee, whose last name is unapologetically appropriate as he is definitely a cutie. And he's a good police officer, too, devoted to protecting and serving and keeping the island safe from dastardly crooks.

"Um, no, I haven't," I say, mentally kicking myself. "But I will ask him."

Marty frowns. "See that you do."

"Absolutely!" I promise. "And I will get lots of detailed details!"

Marty doesn't look convinced. "You better do better, Sophia. Or you'll be out the door."

Chapter 2

Of course, Marty is right about the diamond heist story.

I didn't give my readers enough details. But not because I didn't want to. But because I couldn't give them more details. Not only did the responding officer refuse to speak to me, but the diamond store owner, Mr. Ephraim Beauchamp, was too distraught to give me an interview.

But I promised Marty I would get more details and that's exactly what I plan to do. I'm going to head over to the diamond store, which is called Beauchamp & Daughters Fine Jewelry, and talk to Mr. Beauchamp. Hopefully, he's gotten past the trauma of being robbed. Hopefully, I won't have to implore or beseech him to give me an interview, however, I'm not above begging, if I have to. After all, I can't get shipped out. I have to shape up. I have to get off probation and become a senior reporter. And yes, these do seem like tall orders, but I plan to fill them.

Hopefully.

Anyhoo.

Grabbing my purse, my cell phone, and my car keys, I leave the office and cross the parking lot, heading toward my red JEEP.

Overhead, thick charcoal-colored clouds swirl like smoke in a cauldron, trapping the heat. The atmosphere is heavy with humidity, but the gusty sea breezes keep it from being too oppressive.

After using the key fob to unlock the car, I open the driver's door, and—

"Hey, girl, where you headed?"

Recognizing the familiar voice, which is full of sass, I smile and glance down.

Callie, the Calico cat, lifts a paw in greeting before she leaps up into the JEEP, jumps across the center console, and settles herself into the passenger's seat.

I hop into the car and close the door. "Remember that story I did about the diamond shop that got robbed?"

Bobbing her head, Callie says, "Let me guess, your boss didn't like it?"

Starting the ignition, I shake my head. "He says the story needs more details. And he's right."

"Girl, that man stay giving you the blues."

Nodding, I say, "And the reds, and the oranges, and the greens, and the purples, and—"

"Okay, okay, I get it, sis," says the cat. "What's his problem?"

I shift into reverse and back out of the parking space. "His problem is my writing."

"I thought it was getting better," says Callie, licking her left hind leg.

"So, did I, but ..."

"Girl, I meant to ask you," says the cat, licking her right hind leg. "What happened to that story about the dead body that washed up on the beach?"

"Didn't I tell you about that?" I ask, steering out of the lot and onto the main road.

"If you had told me, would I be asking you what happened?"

"No, I suppose you wouldn't," I conclude, merging into the morning traffic. "Well, it was sort of a bust."

"Explain," demands the cat. "Or expound. Or extrapolate. Tell me what you mean. How was it a bust?"

Sighing, I shake my head. "The dead body on the beach turned out to be a blowup doll."

"A blowup doll?"

"Turns out, someone stole a blowup doll," I tell her. "The note was supposed to say, you'll never see your doll again ... not you'll never see your dog again. It was a crazy prank involving a group of university students."

"Girl, you humans worry me sometimes," says the cat as she licks her fur. "Some of you don't have the sense God gave a nanny goat and that's an insult to the nanny goat."

Laughing, I say, "You sound like my grandma."

"Anyway," says the cat. "I need you to drop me off at the Royal St. Mateo hotel."

Curious, I ask, "What's going on at the Royal St. Mateo hotel?"

"Miss me with all that interrogation." The cat rises to all fours. "But if you must know ... I'm having breakfast with the tomcat."

"Things are heating up between you two, it seems," I say.

The cat stares at me. "Girl, whatever. You know I can't be tied down. And anyway ... "

"What ...?"

The cat looks away from me. "Well, considering my ... situation ..."

"You mean ... the catnesia?"

A month ago, when Callie chose me to be her human—while making it unabashedly clear that she is absolutely *not* my cat—she admitted that she has catnesia. Basically, it's a feline form of amnesia. Callie can't remember anything about her life before I rescued her from a Seagrape tree. She's anxious and curious about her past, particularly how and why she ended up stuck in a tree. I've agreed to help her investigate, even though it might mean she's someone else's cat. The thought bothers and saddens me, but I can't be selfish. I want Callie to unlock the secrets of her past.

Bobbing her head, the feline says, "I could wake up one morning and remember that I'm already in a relationship."

Or, she could wake up and remember that she already has a human, I think, but don't say.

Suppressing a sigh, I tell her. "Well, don't worry. We'll figure it out."

Chapter 3

"Good Afternoon, young lady!" exclaims Ephraim Beauchamp, the owner of Beauchamp & Daughters, hurrying around a U-shaped glass display case that dominates the small store. Scurrying up the center aisle, he clasps his hands together and smiles in a way that suggests he can hardly contain his excitement.

He's a little gnome of a man, with large cheeks, kind eyes, and a deep sandy complexion suggestive of Southeast Asian ancestry. Dressed in a three-piece suit the color of fresh raw salmon, he appears both dapper and cartoonish, like a television game show host.

"How may I help you?" asks Mr. Beauchamp, like it's the only thing in the world he wants to do. "Are you looking for a decadent diamond? Maybe a pretty pearl? Perhaps a ravishing ruby? Or an enchanting emerald? How about a sultry sapphire?"

"All of those gems sound absolutely wonderful," I say. "But unfortunately I'm not here to buy anything. My name is Sophie Carter. I'm a reporter from the *Palmchat Gazette*."

Beauchamp smiles. "Ah, Miss Sophie from the *Palmchat Gazette*."

Encouraged, I ask, "You remember me?"

"No, I am afraid not but please tell me if for some reason I should."

"Well, I wanted to interview you for my story when your diamonds were stolen, but you were too upset."

Beauchamp shakes his head. "Yes, it was a distressing time."

"Well, if you're feeling better maybe we could talk now?" I ask. "You see, I need more details about the robbery so I can write a follow-up story."

The store owner nods. "I am doing much better, and you are kind to ask as I have cycled through the stages of grief more than once and again find myself accepting my fate even though I would have thought the police could have caught the crook by now and I worry my diamonds will never be found and returned to me."

"Don't think that way," I tell the jewelry store owner. "You have to believe that you'll get the diamonds back."

"I try not to lose heart," says Beauchamp, sighing. "But it is very disheartening. Although one thing does give me hope."

"What's that?"

"I am quite certain that I know who stole my diamonds," declares Beauchamp.

Shocked, I ask, "Are you serious? Who was it?"

"I do not know their names," says Beauchamp. "But I remember their faces."

"Wait," I say. "*Their* faces? Do you mean that more than one person robbed you?"

Nodding, Beauchamp says, "Alas, I was ambushed by a dastardly duo!"

Flabbergasted, I dig into my purse and grab my phone. "Is it okay if I record you? Just so you're not misquoted or misstated?"

"*D'accord,*" says Beauchamp, waving a hand. "It is fine."

"Tell me more about the people who robbed you," I request.

"It was a man and a woman," says Beauchamp. "They fooled me

into thinking they were a couple who wanted to look at engagement rings. As soon as I began to show them the rings, the woman pulled a gun on me and forced me into my office, where I keep the safe that contains loose diamonds and my most expensive pieces. I should have known they were lying about getting married. She was a stunning woman, a beautiful blonde with lovely blue eyes ... and the man was a troll."

"A troll?" I ask, thinking of a maniacal miscreant lurking under a bridge.

"A toad." Beauchamp shudders, disgust plastered on his face.

Confused, I say, "Wait. Was he a troll? Or a toad? Or—"

"And he smelled like sour goat milk," says Beauchamp, as though he's currently experiencing the offending stench. "He was St. Matean, but with mixed European ancestry, most likely. His eyes were brown and shifty. He could not look me in the eye. He was medium height, but thin and frail. He wore an expensive suit, I could tell, but it hung off his frame. And the tie he wore was atrocious!"

"Atrocious?" I echo.

"Abhorrent!" Beauchamp shudders again.

Perplexed, I say, "Wait. Was the tie atrocious? Or Abhorrent? Or—"

"A gaudy neon green and purple striped tie which clashed violently with the mustard yellow suit," exclaims Beauchamp, his mouth twisted in a scornful scowl.

"Do you have any camera surveillance from that day?" I ask. "Something you can show the police so maybe they can find the people who robbed you."

"There was footage from the day of the robbery," says Beauchamp. "I gave it to the police but they told me that it was too grainy. They could not clearly make out the faces of the couple so they could not identify them."

"Well, that is unfortunate," I say.

"*Zut alors,*" declares Beauchamp. "That it is ..."

Clearing my throat, I ask, "So, once the couple forced you into your office, the woman demanded that you open the safe?"

Beauchamp nods. "At first, I refused but the woman made it clear that she would shoot me and use my cold dead thumb to open the safe if I did not comply with her wicked instructions. And so, I placed my thumb over the sensor."

"Your cold dead ... *thumb?*" I ask.

"The safe has a biometric entry feature," says Beauchamp. "Only my left thumbprint will open the safe."

"Do the police have any leads?" I ask.

Tsking, Beauchamp says, "After the police were unable to identify the culprits from my video surveillance, they seemed to no longer care about my case."

"That's terrible," I say. "But all is not lost."

Giving me a dubious look, he says, "All may not be lost, but my diamonds certainly are."

"Well, maybe I can help ..."

Frowning, Mr. Beauchamp asks, "You? How?"

"Well, I'm going to write another story about the robbery," I say. "I have to, or I'll be fired."

"*Sacre bleu!*" Beauchamp looks stricken. "Fired?"

Nodding, I say, "My manager put me on probation last month. He says my writing is not up to par. And I don't have enough details in my articles. He has promised to ship me out if I don't shape up. Anyway. Maybe someone who knows something about the theft of your diamonds will read the story and contact the cops about what they know."

His expression skeptical, Mr. Beauchamp says, "Perhaps, but—"

A muted two-tone chime arrests the store owner's attention, pulling his gaze away from me. I glance in the same direction. Three people—tourists, if I had to guess, judging from their casual attire of walking shorts, T-shirts, and sandals—enter the jewelry store.

"Customers," says Beauchamp, his frown turning upside down. "I must attend to them."

"Oh, of course," I say. "Thanks for talking to me!"

"It was my pleasure, Ms. Sophie," says Mr. Beauchamp. "Blessings to you and good luck with your article!"

Chapter 4

"Got a minute?"

I knock on Marty's door, which is half opened, and poke my head inside.

It's a little after nine in the morning. Normally, around this time, I would be enjoying a cup of steaming hot mango and spearmint tea with cinnamon donut holes from Too A Tea, one of my favorite tea cafes, but I'm anxious to find out what Marty thinks about my diamond heist follow-up article.

After my visit to Mr. Beauchamp, I went back to the *Palmchat Gazette*, wrote the story, and then emailed it to Marty. He gave me a few revisions, which I fixed, and then he approved it for initial publication on the paper's website. Unfortunately, his feedback was mostly grammatical so I have no idea if he liked my writing. Was my word choice okay? How about my sentence flow? Did I hook the readers with a great lead paragraph?

"Not really," gripes Marty, not bothering to turn from his computer, where he pecks at the keyboard with his thick, sausage-like fingers.

"How about a second?" I inquire.

Exhaling, Marty says, "What do you need, Sophia?"

"Just wondering what you thought about my diamond heist follow-up story?" I ask, slipping into his office.

Dragging a hand down his florid face, Marty swivels toward me.

I drop down into the chair in front of his desk. "Was it much better than my last few stories?"

Sitting back, Marty rubs the short, spiky stubble clinging to his chin. "I wouldn't say much better."

"Kinda better?" I hope.

Marty hems and then haws.

Confused, I ask, "Sorta better?"

Marty haws and then hems.

Worried, I ask, "A little bit better?"

Marty says, "Less horrible."

"Oh ... " I say, my gaze dropping to my hands as I try not to feel deflated.

"Anyway, since you're here," begins Marty, "I'm going to give you another chance to prove that you can be sorta better or kinda better, although I doubt you'll prove me wrong, but I need someone to cover a story and there's no other reporter to do it, so you're it."

"Great!" I say, smiling, although I don't feel so great. I feel like I was Marty's best bad choice or something, but I do need to show Marty that my writing and reporting are getting kinda, sorta better. The only way I'm going to prove that Marty is wrong about me, and I do have that elusive "it" he thinks I'll never have, is to cover more stories and write more articles.

"Around seven this morning," says Marty, "cops responded to a report of a dead body in the Tobacco Coast neighborhood."

"How horrific!" I say, shuddering.

Marty says, "You need to get lots of details."

"Absolutely!"

"And witness statements."

"Absolutely!"

"And some sort of comment from the police. Understand?"

"Absolutely!" I say.

Scowling at me, Marty asks, "You know any other words besides 'absolutely'?"

Giving him a winning smile, I say, "Absolutely!"

Several moments later—after tea and donut holes, which I need for fortification, galvanization, and tenacity—I stride briskly across the employee parking lot toward my JEEP.

Despite the fact that Marty only gave me the Tobacco Coast Murder case because he had no other choice, I am resolved to do a great job. Marty thinks I'm hopeless, I know. He doubts my skill, my abilities, and my critical thinking. He can't believe I have a journalism degree—which I most certainly do—and thinks I only got the job at the *Palmchat Gazette* satellite office in St. Mateo because I'm good friends with the publisher's wife, Vivian Thomas-Bronson—which I certainly did, but …

Wait.

That's not exactly true.

Well, I am good friends with Vivian, but she didn't give me a job that I don't deserve. And, as a matter of fact, Vivian didn't give me the job. Her husband, the publisher, Leo Bronson, hired me. And to tell you the truth—which I always aim to do as it is my goal to be a prudent and ethical journalist—Vivian didn't even think I should have this job, so …

Wait.

Well, actually, that is true, but—

"Girl, are you okay?"

Startled, I glance to my left.

Callie the Calico sits on the hood of my JEEP, licking her front paw.

"Oh, hey, Callie," I say, chuckling. "I'm fine."

"Girl, are you sure?" asks the cat. "You've been staring into space for the last ten minutes."

Shaking my head, I say, "I was just thinking."

"About what?"

"I got a new story to cover," I say, shielding my eyes from the bright, harsh mid-morning St. Mateo sun.

"Not another blowup doll on the beach, I hope," says the cat.

"Dead body in Tobacco Coast," I say. "And, of course, Marty has demanded that I get details, and witness statements, and comments from the cops, oh my!"

Callie hisses at me. "Girl, it is too early in the morning for a Wizard of Oz reference."

I tilt my head. "Is it?"

After giving me a look, Callie goes back to licking her paw.

"Anyway, I have to prove to Marty that I'm a good investigative reporter."

"Girl, I thought you had already done that," says the cat.

"So did I," I say, shrugging. "But Marty wasn't impressed by my diamond heist follow-up story."

"Why not?" asks Callie, rising to all fours. "Didn't you have details, and witness statements, and comments from the cops?"

"Oh no!" I lament, smacking my palm against my forehead.

"What is it?" demands Callie, hissing and arching her back.

"That's what I forgot," I say, groaning. "No wonder Marty told me my story was only less horrible than usual. I should have called the detective assigned to the case to get more information."

Callie says, "Well, maybe you could—"

"Sophie ...? Who are you talking to?"

I freeze.

The feeling of ice-cold snow flurries fluttering through me is not only due to the familiar voice of my coworker, Clark Kent, even though Clark's voice usually makes me shiver.

I'm also paralyzed because I'm having a conversation with a Calico cat.

Not that I can tell Clark that.

Because not only would he not believe me, but I wouldn't be able to prove it. Callie is a talking cat who only talks to me. And I'm a human who only talks to her. Translation: Callie and I can understand each other, but I can't talk to any other cats. Similarly, she can't converse with any other humans.

Mentally kicking myself, I take a deep breath and face Clark.

Of course, the deep breath doesn't help.

Because Clark is one of those guys who leaves you breathless. He's super handsome. A dreamboat, as my grandma would say. He's tall, muscular, and has mesmerizing green-gray eyes.

Clearing my throat, I give Clark a smile and then say, "Oh, hey … how are you?"

"Good," says Clark, nodding. "How are you?"

"Fabulous!"

Eyes slightly narrowed, Clark asks, "Um, just now … were you talking to your cat?"

"Talking to my cat?" I echo, my voice high and squeaky.

Pointing a finger around me, Clark says, "Your cat?"

"Girl, what cat are you talking about talking to?" asks Callie. "Did he ask you about talking to me? Because I'm not your cat."

Executing a somewhat graceful pirouette, I face Callie. "Yes, I know that …" I whisper.

"You know what?" asks Clark.

I face Clark again. "Well, um … I know that Callie is not my cat."

"Set him straight, sis," says the cat, behind me.

Clark crosses his arms across his chest and frowns in a way that makes him even cuter. "If she's not your cat then why did you give her a name?"

"I didn't name her," I say. "I found out that her name is Callie, but I don't remember how … anyway, I gotta get going. Marty wants me to cover a murder in Tobacco Coast."

Clark says, "He wants me to take photos."

"Want a ride to the crime scene together?" I ask, hoping to steer Clark away from his questions about Callie.

"That'd be great," says Clark.

"Well, since you and your cute coworker are leaving," says Callie, "guess I'll bounce. See ya later, sis."

I turn back to the cat and wave. "Bye!"

After Callie scampers away, I face Clark again. The look in his green-gray eyes is curious, suspicious, and slightly amusing.

"What is it?" I ask, hoping I look innocent and not as though I just said goodbye to a feline.

"If she's not your cat," says Clark. "Then who does she belong to?"

"I have no idea," I admit, using my key fob to unlock the JEEP doors. "That's what I need to find out."

"She doesn't have a collar?"

I shake my head. "No."

Walking around to the passenger side, Clark says, "Is she microchipped?"

I frown. "Microchipped?"

Clark says, "Lots of people have microchips embedded into their pets. Then if the pets are lost or stolen, it's easier to find the owner."

Inside the JEEP, I turn the ignition, then glance at Clark. "How could I find out if she's got a microchip?"

Fiddling with his camera, Clark says, "Just take her to a vet. They should have the equipment to scan for a chip."

Shifting into reverse, I ponder Clark's suggestion. It's a great idea. Probably the best way to find out who Callie belongs to. And yet I still don't like the idea of finding Callie's owner, but if someone is out there worried about her, and looking for her, then ...

Well, that person deserves to have their cat back, don't they?

Chapter 5

Despite its name, the neighborhood of Tobacco Coast is not on the island's coast.

It's actually nowhere near the ocean. The working-class blue-collar enclave of small, chattel homes is in the island's interior, surrounded by lush rainforest. The area got its name because the houses were built near an old, abandoned tobacco plantation.

With Clark's help, I navigate the streets to the crime scene—a lavender house with white trim blocked by half a dozen St. Mateo police cars. After parking my JEEP along the gravel-lined shoulder, Clark and I exit the vehicle and make our way across a thin strip of road. I grab my *Palmchat Gazette* press credentials from my cross body as I survey the chaotic scene. Cops mill about, talking to each other while forensic technicians walk into and out of the lavender house.

Hordes of neighbors cluster on the tiny lawns in front of the houses on either side of the victim's home. Many of them hold up cell phones as they talk and point and nod and shake their heads.

"I'm going to see if I can get some shots of the body," announces Clark.

"Okay, I'm going to—"

I trail off as I notice Officer Noah Cuetee, standing on the porch, talking to another deputy.

"Going to ... what?"

"Talk to Officer Cuetee," I say, pushing strands of my corkscrew curls from my face.

"Officer ... *cutie?*" asks Clark, smirking slightly as he raises an eyebrow.

Rolling my eyes, I say, "Believe it, or not, Cuetee is the officer's last name. And you should believe it—Clark Kent."

Frowning, Clark shakes his head. "Don't remind me."

I laugh as Clark jogs away, heading toward the entrance of the lavender house. As Clark hurries up the steps onto the porch, Officer Cuetee glances toward me.

His lovely smile sets off what feels like a million butterflies in my stomach.

As I smile back and wave, Officer Cuetee leaves the porch and strides toward me, looking very much like a dreamboat, as my grandma would say.

Officially, he's my anonymous, confidential police source in the St. Mateo police department. I met him last month, and he was very instrumental in helping me as I investigated the case of the vicious murder of my coworker, a reporter named Ruth Rice. Officer Cuetee is also a very good friend. We have lots in common, including an affinity for flavored tea and donut holes. And although we've seen each other socially, I wouldn't say that we're dating. But I do like him. He's swoon-worthy and would probably make a great boyfriend. Not that I'm looking for a boyfriend right now. I have to prove to Marty that I have "it," get off probation, and become a Senior Investigative Reporter. Alas, I just don't have time for a love life right now.

"Hey, Sophie!" greets Officer Cuetee. "How are you?"

"Great!" I say, trying not to get lost in his Caribbean blue eyes.

"How are you?"

"Doing well," he says before his smile falters. "Despite the circumstances, that is ..."

"Speaking of the circumstances, which are dire," I agree, removing my cell phone from my cross-body. "But what can you tell me about what happened here?"

"We got a call around seven this morning about a woman found dead in her bedroom," says Officer Cuetee. "She's been identified as Cynthia Snowpearce."

"How did she die?"

"Strangled to death," says Officer Cuetee.

I shudder. "Gruesome."

"The medical examiner said there were ligature marks around her neck indicative of asphyxiation due to strangulation," continues Officer Cuetee. "He believes the killer may have used some type of cord. The crime scene techs are still collecting evidence."

"Any suspects?" I ask.

"Not yet," says Officer Cuetee. "We're trying to find the person who reported the crime. There was no one at the home when we arrived."

"Was the person who called in the murder a man or a woman?"

"According to dispatch," says Officer Cuetee, "it was a man."

"Doesn't dispatch track the number and location of the phone used when people call 911?" I ask.

Officer Cuetee says, "I'm sure the detective will get that information. And speaking of the detective ..."

Noticing that Officer Cuetee is looking over my head at something behind me, I glance back over my shoulder.

A low groan escapes my lips.

About fifteen feet away, standing near a small lemon tree, are two men in dark linen suits. One of them seems to be in his mid-fifties, with a pained, yet patient expression on his slightly careworn face.

The other man is tall, handsome, well-built, and ... giving me a look that could absolutely kill.

But I'm not surprised.

The grumpy guy is Detective Richland Francois.

He and his four brothers are known across the Caribbean as the Francois Brothers, a group of tough, intelligent lawmen known for their ability to solve murder cases. This skill was apparently inherited from their father and grandfather, also detectives with sterling reputations in law enforcement.

Detective Richland Francois is also known for his unabashed and irrevocable dislike of the media.

Which explains why he's frowning at me.

Glancing back at Officer Cuetee, I bite my lower lip. "We probably shouldn't let him see us talking."

"You're probably right," says Officer Cuetee, a flicker of worry flashing across his face. "But he's already seen us, so ..."

"So ... he doesn't know what we were talking about," I say.

"You're right," says Officer Cuetee, smiling. "I could be asking you if you want to meet for tea this Saturday morning."

"That's true!" I say, smiling back. "And I could be telling you that I'd love to meet for tea this coming Saturday."

"I'll text you the details," says Officer Cuetee, and then he heads back to the porch to rejoin the other cops.

"Thought I'd save you the trouble ..."

The low, gruff voice, behind me, kills every single one of those butterflies I felt when Officer Cuetee smiled at me earlier.

I take a deep breath and turn to face Detective Francois.

Cowering beneath his impressive height, I stumble back a bit and in the process, drop my phone. Feeling like a complete klutz, I bend over and grab the phone. With a nervous giggle—completely unprofessional, trust me, I know—I straighten and clear my throat, trying to get myself together, which at this point seems to be a hopeless and futile endeavor.

"Detective François!" I say, affecting a cheerful attitude and sunny disposition, one which I hope will eliminate the furrow between his brows. "How are you today?"

The detective's scowl deepens.

"Yes, well ..." I clear my throat again. "You mentioned that you wanted to save me some trouble?"

"As you know, it is not my custom to speak to the press about active investigations," begins Francois.

"I know that very well," I confirm. "Customarily, as you pointed out, you don't—"

"However instead of saying no comment," interrupts the detective, "I'll say this ..."

A flicker of hope sparks within me at the thought of the detective actually giving me a statement. Quickly, I check my phone to make sure the recording app is still working.

"Yes ..." I prompt, wondering what Francois will say. Of course, I don't expect him to give me any inside information or off-the-record details, but he might tell me—

"I have nothing to say about this case at this time," says Francois. "And furthermore, I will have nothing to say about this case at any time in the future. So ... I thought I would save you the trouble of pestering me about a comment for your article."

As the detective turns, rather unceremoniously and with no salutations, I mumble under my breath, "Gee, thanks ... you really shouldn't have ... "

Chapter 6

"Aliens ..." says Mr. Buford Stanley, giving me a shrewd look over the rim of the coffee mug he sips from.

"Aliens?" I repeat, confused as I stare at the tall, gangly man dressed in a dingy karate uniform.

After Detective Francois systematically and with malice, and forethought—though it would probably be hard for me to prove that —crushed my hopes and dashed my dreams of getting an actual statement from him, I took a moment to feel sorry for myself.

But the moment didn't last very long.

Maybe a minute or two.

Recalling my promise to Marty to get detailed details for my story, I focused on the neighbors clustered on the lawn next door and walked over to a circle of withered old guys, and introduced myself. Initially, they expressed their shock and surprise that such a horrid, heinous crime would take place in their neighborhood. Tobacco Coast, according to them, is a quiet, simple place where decent folks do right by each other and make sure to keep their lawns mowed.

One of the men—a Mr. Morrison—revealed his position as

president of the Neighborhood Association and assured me it was his mission to make sure the lawns were well-maintained.

"We have the jungle in our backyards," he's explained. "We don't need the jungle in our front yards, too."

"No, certainly not," I'd agreed.

"Ms. Snowpearce kept her lawn looking mighty fine," Mr. Morrison had said, shaking his head. "That's why what happened to her is such a shame! Now that she's dead, who's going to cut the yard?"

"I'll bet you it's going to be nothing but weeds in two weeks' time," predicted another man, his tone dire.

While Mr. Morrison lamented the house being sold to people who might not have a lawn mower, hedge clippers, or sufficient knowledge of fertilizer, I asked if anyone had any idea about who would want to kill Cynthia Snowpearce.

That was when Mr. Stanley beckoned me away from the others to tell me his theory.

"You mean aliens like ... extra-terrestrials?"

"I don't know nothing about no terrestrials," says Mr. Stanley. "I'm not into all that. Some folks are, and that's their business, but what I'm telling you is aliens killed that woman. I will bet money on it."

As I wonder how to respond, I get the feeling that Mr. Stanley is sipping something a lot stronger than hot java. "Okay, so ... well, these ... aliens ... how do you know they killed Ms. Snowpearce?"

"Because they told me."

"They told you?" I ask. "You spoke to them?"

Taking another sip from his mug, Mr. Stanley says, "Had a very lengthy conversation with them. Very lengthy. Nice people."

Perplexed, I say, "But ... you think they killed Ms. Snowpearce?"

"Oh, I know they did."

"And yet you think they're nice?" I ask.

"Sometimes good people do bad things," says Mr. Stanley.

"I see," I say, even though I don't. "Well, did the aliens tell you why they killed Ms. Snowpearce?"

"Is this old fool telling you nonsense about aliens killing Ms. Snowpearce?" bellows a large, rotund man wearing an orange terry cloth robe and matching house slippers. He ambles toward us, sipping from a mug that says *World's Best Bullfighter*. I am absolutely curious, but I decide not to ask.

"Who are you calling an old fool?" demands Mr. Stanley, nostrils flaring, eyes flashing. "I'm younger than you! And I have all my faculties!"

Of course, I beg to differ, but I decide not to dispute Mr. Stanley's passionate declaration.

Instead, I turn to the man in the orange terry cloth robe. "And your name sir?"

"Theodore O'Reilly," he says. "I live next door to Ms. Snowpearce."

"And do you have any idea who might have killed her?" I ask.

"Well, I know it wasn't aliens!" says O'Reilly, expelling a hearty laugh.

"You don't know nothing!" grumbles Mr. Stanley as he stomps away.

Anxious for a rational, logical theory, I ask Mr. O'Reilly, "Who do you think killed Ms. Snowpearce? You know, if it wasn't ... aliens."

Mr. O'Reilly takes a sip of whatever is in his cup, and then says, "You ask me, I say it was the jungle creature."

"I'm sorry ..." I start, not sure I've heard him correctly. "Did you say—"

"The jungle creature," says Mr. O'Reilly, nodding.

"The jungle creature?" I repeat, my hopes for a logical, rational theory fading quickly.

"The jungle creature lives in the jungle," says Mr. O'Reilly.

And where else would he live, I think but decide not to say.

"He's a shy, reclusive creature who keeps to himself," says the man, after another sip of what I am sure is some sort of liquid hallucinogenic. "He does not bother anybody. He wants to be left alone, in solitude, to contemplate his fate."

"His fate?" I ask though I suspect I shouldn't. I don't want to encourage Mr. O'Reilly's delusions, and yet I find myself curious about this jungle creature, who I am sure is not real. Nevertheless ...

"He must contend with the soul-crushing reality of being part man, part iguana, and part jaguar," explains Mr. O'Reilly. "It is a fate that was thrust upon him."

"In what way?" I ask, even though, again, I probably shouldn't. Nevertheless ...

"There is no proof of this," says Mr. O'Reilly, voice lowered, eyes darting suspiciously, "but I believe he was the victim of secret, unauthorized medical experiments carried out by some shady government organization."

"I see ..." I say, even though I don't.

"Despite his penchant for solitude," says Mr. O'Reilly, "the jungle creature does get lonely, at times, and longs for a friend."

"A friend?"

"He is partial to hamsters," says the man in the orange terry cloth robe.

"Hamsters?"

"He seeks to make friends with the small animals," he explains. "Ms. Snowpearce had a hamster. I think the jungle creature broke into Ms. Snowpearce's home, not with the intent of purloining any of her items, but to make friends with her hamster."

"If the jungle creature wanted to make friends with the hamster, then why did he kill Cynthia Snowpearce?" I ask, finding it hard to believe that the question actually came from my mouth.

"I don't believe the jungle creature intended to kill Cynthia," says

O'Reilly, then takes another sip from his cup. "I believe she discovered him in her home, became terrified, and attacked him. I believe he tried to communicate his intent to befriend the hamster, however, due to his horrific appearance, Cynthia couldn't understand that he meant her no harm. The jungle creature, under attack, had no choice but to defend himself, and thus, he was forced, through no fault of his own, to kill Cynthia."

"You really think the jungle creature wasn't at fault?" I ask. "I mean, he broke into Cynthia's house. She was defending herself against him."

"Well, that certainly is one way to look at it," allows O'Reilly.

"Have you told the police about the jungle creature?" I ask.

Shaking his head, O'Reilly says, "Oh no! I wouldn't want to get the jungle creature in trouble!"

"But don't you want justice for Cynthia?"

"Of course, I do!" declares O'Reilly, adding a mournful sigh. "Alas, not at the expense of the jungle creature who I fear will be hunted and killed—or, worse, experimented on again—if the police find out what he did."

"But suppose the jungle creature didn't kill Cynthia Snowpearce?" I suggest. "After all, you don't know for sure that he killed her, right? You only suspect him."

Stroking his chin, O'Reilly says, "Again, that certainly is another way to look at it."

"The jungle creature might be innocent," I say.

"What type of ridiculous tomfoolery are you telling this young lady Theodore?"

The voice, which is brash and gravelly, but unmistakably female, startles me, and I spin around—making myself just a tad dizzy in the process—to face a harried-looking woman wearing a T-shirt, jeans, and flip-flops. She smokes a cigarette and her wiry salt-and-pepper hair sticks out in every direction on her head.

His chest puffed out, Mr. O'Reilly, his jowls shaking, says, "I beg your pardon!"

The older woman sucks on her cigarette and then blows the smoke directly into O'Reilly's face. "Scram!"

Sputtering curses, Mr. O'Reilly waddles away.

Exhaling, the woman says, "You want to know who killed Cynthia? I'll tell you."

"And your name?" I ask, checking the recording app again.

"Lotty Dotty."

Wary, I glance at her. "Lotty … Dotty?"

"Charlotte Dotty," she says, then takes another pull on the cigarette.

"But people call you Lotty?"

Turning her head to blow the smoke away from me, Lotty Dotty nods and says, "Who did O'Reilly say killed Cynthia? Aliens?"

"No, no … not aliens," I say. "Mr. Stanley said aliens. Mr. O'Reilly said the jungle creature."

Lotty Dotty barks a laugh that sends her into a coughing fit.

"Are you okay?" I ask. The woman sounds like Callie when she's struggling to hack up a furball. "Do you need some water, or …"

"Oh, no, honey …" Lotty Dotty takes a long, deep breath as the coughs subside. "What I need is to stop smoking, but anyway, wasn't aliens or a jungle creature who killed Cynthia. I swear, those old coots need to stop drinking whatever it is they have in those mugs."

"You know I was thinking the same thing," I confide, voice lowered. "What's in those mugs anyway?"

"Some kind of bug juice," says Lotty Dotty. "I'm serious. It's some kind of elixir they make from cicadas. All the old farts around here swear it's a miracle cure. And that may be true. Good for the body. Bad for the mind. Anyway, I think Cynthia's boyfriend killed her."

"What's her boyfriend's name?" I ask, grateful for a real lead.

"Willie Peters," says Lotty Dotty. "He and Cynthia had been

arguing a lot recently. She told me he'd threatened her. Told her he would kill her. Now, Cynthia was what you might call a tough girl, so she wasn't really worried. Thought Willie was just trying to scare her. Now that she's dead, I'm thinking Willie Peters made good on his threat."

Chapter 7

"Word on the street is the dead woman's hamster knows who killed her ..."

The words, coming out of nowhere, startle me, even though I recognize Callie's voice.

Nevertheless, I scream.

Callie hisses. "Girl, what is your problem!"

Clamping my mouth shut, I shift the JEEP into park and twist around the stare toward the backseat.

Licking her fur, the cat says, "Listen, sis ... in the future, miss me with all that hollering, okay? Cats have very sensitive ears!"

"How about, in the future, you miss me with showing up in my JEEP unannounced?"

"Girl, don't get an attitude with me because you leave the top off your JEEP," says Callie, staring at me.

Glancing up, I see nothing but the afternoon St. Mateo sky, which is streaked with wispy clouds that remind me of pink and baby blue cotton candy. Sighing, I shake my head. "Sorry, sorry. Didn't mean to be snippy, I just ..."

"You just what?" asks Callie, leaping into the front passenger seat. "What's the matter? You look upset."

I cut the ignition. "Well, that's because I am upset. I don't have any good, viable leads for the story Marty sent me this morning."

After leaving the crime scene in Tobacco Coast, Clark and I drove back to the *Palmchat Gazette* offices. While Clark went off to organize the photos he'd taken of Cynthia Snowpearce's dead body, I wrote the first draft of my story. I decided to headline the article, WOMAN STRANGLED TO DEATH IN TOBACCO COAST. The body of the article detailed the who, what, when, where, and how. Obviously, I didn't know why, and the last thing I wanted to write was anything about the ridiculous, illogical theories put forth by Mr. Stanley and Mr. O'Reilly. I emailed the draft to Marty, but he didn't get back to me because he was at a meeting on the other side of the island.

Suffice it to say, I'm worried about what Marty will think.

Will he think my writing is getting progressively better? Or abysmally worse?

"You're talking about that dead body found in Tobacco Coast?"

"Right." I nod. "I promised Marty I would get detailed details, and I did, but the details are so ridiculous. The woman who was killed—Cynthia Snowpearce—had the craziest neighbors. They think she was killed by aliens. Or, some jungle creature, or—"

"Girl, did you just hear me?" asks the cat. "And more importantly, did you understand what I said?"

"Sorry," I say, sheepish. "Tell me again."

After a slight hiss of annoyance, Callie says, "Word on the street is the dead woman's hamster knows who killed her."

Confused, I say, "Wait. The word on what street?"

"Girl, the name of the street doesn't matter," says Callie. "The point is that the dead woman, Cynthia Snowpearce, had a pet hamster."

"A pet hamster …" I echo, recalling my conversation with Mr. O'Reilly.

"And I heard the hamster saw the murder," says the cat.

I glance at the cat. "Heard from who?"

The feline licks her left paw. "This gossipy bird who's always all up in everybody's business. Anyway, the bird is friends with the hamster."

"And you're friends with the bird?"

"Not friends," says Callie. "I needed some information from her about a situation I'm dealing with."

"What kind of information?" I ask. "What situation are you dealing with?"

"Girl, will you focus?" demands Callie. "We need to talk to that hamster."

"Right, I know that," I say, debating whether or not to tell the cat what I was thinking. Does the situation she referred to have anything to do with her catnesia?

"According to the bird," says Callie. "The hamster heard the dead woman arguing with some guy. And then the guy killed her. The hamster said it was horrible. Apparently, she was choked to death with a purple and neon green striped tie."

"Interesting …" I muse, again thinking about the conversation I had with Mr. O'Reilly.

The cat asks, "What's interesting?"

"When I was interviewing witnesses at the crime scene," I begin, "I talked to a man who mentioned Cynthia Snowpearce's pet hamster. I thought it was crazy because he claimed some jungle creature wanted to make friends with the hamster."

"A jungle creature?"

Shaking my head, I say, "Don't ask."

"Don't worry, girl, I won't," says the cat. "I've already come to terms with the fact that some of you humans don't have the sense

God gave a Billy goat. Anyway, the thing we need to do now is talk to that hamster."

"You're right," I agree. "And speaking of things we need to do ..."

Callie tilts her head as she stares at me.

"You and I need to go and see a vet ..."

Chapter 8

"A vet ...?" Callie hisses and then moves her head back from me. "Why do we need to see a vet? Wait. Girl, are you confused? Do you mean that you need to see a doctor? Is it your head? Are you going back into the coma?"

"No, no ..." I reassure the cat. "I don't need to see a doctor. You and I need to go to a vet."

"But why?" asks Callie. "The only reason animals go to see vets is when they're sick and there is nothing wrong with me."

I tilt my head and give her a look. "You have selective catnesia."

"Oh, well ..." The cat licks her fur. "Other than that ..."

"*That* is why we need to go to the vet."

"*What* is why we need to go to the vet?"

"The selective catnesia," I say.

"The vet is not going to be able to cure my selective catnesia," says Callie.

"Probably not," I agree. "But, the vet can determine if you have been microchipped."

The cat shrinks back from me again. "Microchipped?"

After explaining to Callie how and why microchips are embedded into animals, I say, "So, if you have a microchip, we can find out who your human is."

"You're my human," insists Callie.

"Yes, that's true," I say. "But, I mean … the human you really belong to, you know? I mean, you said yourself that you might have an owner somewhere. Maybe you got lost and this person is looking for you."

"I don't know, girl …" says Callie, turning her head to lick her shoulder.

"What don't you know?"

"I highly doubt I would have consented to being microchipped," says Callie.

"I don't think you would have had a choice," I say. "I think your human would have taken you to the vet and had the procedure done."

"Without my permission?" Callie hisses. "That's a violation of my privacy and basic feline rights."

Confused, I ask, "Cats have … rights?"

Jumping to all fours, Callie says, "I have the right to go wherever I want to go without being tracked like a cat burglar."

Worried that Callie might work herself into psycho mode, I say, "The microchip isn't to track you … okay, well, it is, but … only if you get lost. So you can be returned to your owner."

"I'm not going to the vet," declares Callie.

"But, Callie—"

"Forget it, sis," says Callie. "I said what I said. I'm not going to the vet."

"Why don't you want to go to the vet?" I ask, confused by her staunch refusal.

"Because I don't trust vets," says the cat. "Animals go in and they don't come out."

"What?"

"My friend Blanca went to the vet a few weeks ago," says Callie.

"Her human took her because she was having stomach troubles. She went to the vet to get some medicine. But no one has seen her since then."

Troubled, I say, "Well, maybe she's at home recuperating, or—"

"That vet did something to Blanca," insists Callie. "Something that made her disappear. That's not going to happen to me."

"But, Callie, when we go to the vet, I'll be with you the entire time," I promise. "I won't let the vet do anything bad to you, or—"

"I am not going to the vet!" Callie howls and hisses at me.

"Callie, calm down!" I reach toward the cat.

She swats my hand away, hisses again, and then scampers out of the JEEP, leaping from the passenger window down to the ground.

"Callie!" I jump out of the JEEP and hurry around the front of the vehicle. I'm hoping to catch Callie before she runs off. I want to apologize to her. Tell her I didn't mean to upset her. Assure her that we won't go to the vet if she doesn't want to. Somehow, someway, we'll figure out who she might belong to …

But I'm not fast enough.

Callie is already several yards away, running like all nine of her lives depend upon it.

Chapter 9

"So, I was thinking about my Tobacco Coast murder story," I began, blowing steam from my cup of pear and hibiscus tea.

"What were you thinking about it?" asks Clark, taking a sip of his coffee.

The two of us are sitting in the *Palmchat Gazette* breakroom, enjoying some time away from the mid-morning grind.

"Well, not surprisingly, Marty wants another follow-up," I say, recalling the conversation with my boss two days ago. Marty's feedback wasn't exactly positive, but neither was it scathingly harsh.

"Your writing remains elementary," announced Marty as he paced back and forth behind his desk, squashing his stress ball.

"Elementary?" I echoed.

"You do know that you're not writing for ten-year-olds, right?"

Frowning, I'd said, "But ten-year-olds do read."

Marty had scowled.

I cleared my throat. "Yes, well, um ... you see ..."

"You don't have to always keep it simple, stupid," said Marty.

"Okay ..." I said as I wondered if my boss had just called me stupid. Of course, he could have been executing a droll, clever play on the acronym K.I.S.S., which means "keep it simple, stupid." But, I wasn't sure.

Marty said, "I'd like you to employ a bit of critical thinking and come up with some rational, sound theories as to why Cynthia Snowpearce was killed and who might have wanted her dead."

"A rational, sound theory," I'd repeated, contemplating whether or not an eye-witness account from a traumatized hamster would count as sound and logical—and deciding it wouldn't. "I'll get right on that!"

As it turned out, I didn't get right on it.

And I still haven't.

"My follow-up story is supposed to be about why the victim was killed and who wanted her dead," I tell Clark. "And I'm not quite sure how to figure that out."

"How about you start with figuring out more about the victim," suggests Clark.

"That's a good idea," I say. "If I know more about Cynthia Snowpearce, then I might be able to discover who wanted her dead."

Nodding, Clark says, "Let's do a public record search on her."

Two hours later, Clark shakes his head, and says, "Well, I was not expecting that ..."

"Me, neither," I agree.

The public records search didn't provide any clues but it did reveal a charge for shoplifting when Cynthia Snowpearce was a teenager which gave us the idea to do a criminal records search. Suffice it to say, the criminal search yielded very unexpected revelations.

"It's like pineapple and cucumber tea with sugared lemongrass donut holes," I say.

Clark gapes at me. "Pineapple and cucumber tea with sugared lemongrass donut holes?"

"You don't expect to love those flavor combinations," I tell him. "But, then you do and it's so unexpected."

"Why don't you expect to like pineapple and cucumber tea with sugared lemongrass donut holes?"

"Do you have to ask?"

"Well, I did ask, so I guess I do ..."

I make a face. "Pineapple and cucumber tea with sugared lemongrass donut holes? Doesn't it sound like it would taste like a disaster?"

Clark shrugs. "Actually, it sounds like the reason why I drink coffee."

"And why is that?"

"Because it's uncomplicated."

Nodding, I say, "Unlike Cynthia Snowpearce, whose past is very complicated."

"Can't believe she's a jewel thief," says Clark.

"An alleged jewel thief," I remind him. "She was suspected but never arrested."

As it turned out, Cynthia Snowpearce's name showed up in several law enforcement databases as a person of interest in more than a dozen jewelry heists in the last five years. Police had no evidence connecting her to any of the thefts but she was believed to have been instrumental in carrying out heists across the globe.

Clark says, "Well, if Cynthia Snowpearce was an international jewel thief, then there could be dozens of people who want her dead, from accomplices she betrayed to fences she cheated."

Sighing, I take another sip of tea, and say, "Which doesn't help me in my quest to come up with a suspect."

"What about the boyfriend?" asks Clark. "What was his name?"

"Willie Peters," I say. "I tried to look him up, but believe it or not, there are like, dozens of guys named Willie Peters who live on the island. I didn't know how to start figuring out which one could be Cynthia Snowpearce's boyfriend."

"Who told you about the boyfriend?"

"One of Cynthia's neighbors," I say. "I was hoping she could help me with a description of the boyfriend, or maybe even his contact information, but she's never met him. All she knows about him is what Cynthia told her."

Clark takes a sip of coffee. "Well, I know this will probably suck but you should probably start at the beginning of the list of guys named Willie Peters and call each one of them until you find the right guy."

Making a face, I say, "I was hoping to avoid that."

"Or …" Clark smirks. "You could ask your boyfriend for help."

Frowning, I ask, "What boyfriend?"

"Officer Cuetee," says Clark, his tone teasing. "He might be able to tell you if Detective François has questioned Willie Peters, which is something he would do since—"

"Wait. Wait. Wait." I hold up a hand to stop Clark.

Giving me a look of fake innocence, Clark says, "What?"

"Officer Cuetee is *not* my boyfriend," I insist, trying not to smile as I feel my cheeks warm, although, honestly the fluttery feeling in my chest could be due to Clark's dreamy eyes.

"What is he?"

Feeling a bit smug, I say, "My anonymous source at the St. Mateo police department."

Clark raises his eyebrows. "Is that right?"

I bite my lip. "Somehow I don't think I should have told you that."

"Don't worry," says Clark, giving me another cute smirk. "I won't tell your secret."

Chapter 10

"Hey, girl, hey …"

Recognizing Callie's sassy voice, I turn from the balcony surrounding the small patio connected to my apartment. Before the cat showed up, I was enjoying a late afternoon cup of honey and sweet cream tea as I watched the sunset following a long, and somewhat boring day of fact-checking, researching, and revising articles.

"Hey, girl, hey yourself," I greet the cat, smiling. Since we last spoke, four days ago, I've been worried about her, wondering if I would ever see her again. When my thoughts drifted to the Calico, I experienced pangs of panic and sadness. I still regret pushing the issue of taking Callie to the vet. I should have respected her reluctance—and her fear. I'd been hoping for a chance to tell her how sorry I am for dismissing her feelings, considering what happened to her friend Blanca. Suffice it to say, I'm happy and relieved, to see her.

"Where have you been?" I ask.

Callie stretches out on the chaise lounge. "Here and there …"

I nod. Of course, I'd like her to elaborate but I don't want to upset her. Callie likes her independence and her privacy.

"Anyway I'm here about the hamster," says Callie. "We need to talk to him."

"You're right," I say. "I think, depending on what he has to say, that he could help me with the follow-up story Marty wants me to do. I have to do some investigative reporting and figure out who wanted to kill Cynthia. I've tried looking into her past which, trust me, is sordid, but I still don't have a suspect."

"Well, it's settled," says Callie, rising to all fours.

"What's settled?" I ask, sipping tea.

"Let's go talk to the hamster," says the cat, padding back and forth across the lounge. "Get your keys."

"Wait. What?" I stare at the cat. "You want to go now?"

"What's wrong with now?"

"Well, um, nothing, I suppose, but—"

"Then let's go!"

An hour or so later, Callie and I are standing on the porch of Cynthia Snowpearce's small chattel house in Tobacco Coast.

The sun set thirty minutes ago, leaving behind an indigo sky sprinkled with stars and streaked with lavender and gray clouds. Night animals provide a rhythmic chorus of chirps and buzzing. A gusty breeze cuts through the humidity. The air is fragrant with the smell of earth and lush vegetation.

"Girl, don't stand there like a goat looking at a new gate," pesters the cat. "Let's go inside and find out what the hamster knows."

Excitement sizzles through me, and I nod. "Right, let's do it …"

I reach for the doorknob, twist it, and …

The door doesn't budge.

"What's the matter?" Callie walks to the door, rises on her hind legs, and scratches at the door with her front paws.

My excitement waning, I glance down at her. "The door is locked. Of course, it is. The cops took down the yellow tape, but the house is probably still considered a crime scene."

"So now what?" Back on all fours, the cat walks to me.

Shrugging, I say, "Well, we can't get in, so—"

"Who says we can't get in?"

I give the cat a look. "The door is locked."

"And that's supposed to stop us?" asks Callie.

"Well—"

Before I can finish, the feisty feline leaps off the porch and runs off, heading around the side of the house.

"Callie!" I call after her. "Where are you going? Callie … "

A minute, or two, later when the cat doesn't return, I head down the stairs and make my way around the side of the chattel home. About ten feet ahead, Callie is in front of a window, standing on her hind legs with her paws on the sill.

Hurrying to the cat, I say, "What are you doing?"

Callie turns her head toward me. "We can get in here … "

Staring into her glowing eyes, I approach the window with the utmost caution. "We can get in … where?"

"This window," says Callie. "It's open …"

Moving closer to the window, I can just make out that it seems to be open … but it's a small crack. Maybe about an inch, or inch-and-a-half. Most likely, one of the crime scene techs didn't realize they hadn't closed it all the way.

"No, we cannot go through the window," I say, voice lowered as I glance around. The narrow space between Cynthia Snowpearce's house and the neighbors' home is bathed in darkness. Reaching into my cross-body, I pull out my phone and fumble with it until I access the flashlight.

"Why can't we go through the window?"

Holding the light toward the bottom of the windowsill, I say, "Because we would be breaking into the house."

"Who would know?" asks Callie. "Nobody seems to be around. Maybe her neighbors are asleep. Or watching some dumb television show. You humans love to binge-watch."

"True, but …"

"But … what?" asks Callie. "Listen, we'll be in and out. We'll find out what the hamster knows, thank him for his time, and then we'll leave."

"I don't know …" I say. And, yet, somehow I do know. I know I have to come up with a logical suspect for my follow-up article. I know I have to prove to Marty that I do have "it." I know I have to show all the doubters that I can be a great investigative reporter.

"Girl, we don't have all night," says Callie.

"No, you're right, we don't," I say, bending over to slip my hand beneath the opening above the windowsill. Angling my phone to shine the light on my movements, I push my hand up. With little resistance, the window shoots up.

Callie leaps through the window.

After a deep breath, I follow her, putting my head and upper body through first, then placing one hand on the floor, and then—

My phone falls from my grasp.

"Shoot!" I whisper as it clatters across the floor. Bouncing light illuminates walls and furniture before darkness engulfs the room.

"Girl, what happened to the light?" asks Callie. "Where are you?"

"I dropped my phone," I say, struggling to crawl over the sill and into the house. "I don't know where it went."

"Girl, let me try to find it …"

With one leg inside the house, I drag my other leg through the window, doing a little hopping motion, which disorients me as I put my foot down on something that's soft, springy, and—

Callie screeches loud enough to wake everyone in the neighborhood.

"What? What is it?" I ask, arms outstretched as I try to feel my way in the darkness.

"You stepped on my tail!"

"Oh, my God!" I wail. "Oh, Callie, I'm so sorry!"

"You better be glad I like you, sis," says the cat. "Or, trust me, I would scratch your eyes right out of your head!"

"Callie, I didn't mean it," I say. "When I was coming through the window, I couldn't see, and—"

"I know, I know, it's okay ..."

Seconds later, I feel the cat near my leg. "Oh, Callie, does it hurt?"

"Girl, did you really just ask me that?"

Saddened by her pain, I crouch down. "Can I give you a cuddle?"

"I wouldn't advise it," says the cat. "Now, your phone is about two steps to your left."

Not trusting myself to walk, I bend over onto all fours and scoot to my left. I slide my hands along the dusty wood floor until I feel something hard brush my pinky. I grab the object. It's my phone. Sitting back on my heels, I activate the flashlight.

"Callie ...?" I rise to my feet, using the light to look around the room.

"Over here," says the cat.

Following the sound of her voice, I turn and flash the light in the direction where I heard her.

"Sis, are you trying to blind me?" Callie drops her head and raises her paw over her face.

"Sorry!" I say, angling the flashlight away from her. "Let me find a light switch ..."

Minutes later, the small living room, bathed in the dim, jaundiced light of a bulb in the center of the ceiling, reveals a threadbare loveseat, a scarred and scratched coffee table, and a small television sitting on a wooden console.

"Girl, this place is a dump," exclaims Callie.

"And the crime scene investigators probably didn't help matters," I say, glancing at the dingy walls, stained throw rugs, and thick coating of dust blanketing the hard surfaces.

"Let's hurry and talk to the hamster," says the cat. "I need to get out of here before I catch fleas."

"Where do you think the hamster is?" I ask.

"The dead woman was found in her bedroom, right?" asks the feline. "Let's look there."

Leaving the living room, we travel down a short hall and find the bedroom. I locate the light switch and flip it up. The bedroom is a wreck. Bed sheets and the duvet cover on the floor. The mattress is flipped over. Bureau drawers are pulled from their slots and overturned. Clothes are strewn all over the place.

"This place looks a mess!" I say. "Can't believe the crime scene techs left it this way."

Callie says, "Girl, come look at this."

"What is it?" I follow the cat toward a corner of the room, stepping over small piles of clothes.

On the floor, there's a small cage, the kind you would keep a hamster in, complete with a little running wheel and a food dispenser.

"I don't understand," I say, staring at the empty cage. "Where is the hamster?"

"You tell me."

"You think maybe he got out?" I ask. "He might be hiding somewhere. What's his name? Let's call him."

"Girl, I don't know the hamster," says Callie. "I got my information from that gossipy bird, remember."

"We need to look for him," I say. "I'll check around in here and you—"

"Police! Freeze!"

Chapter 11

"Don't move!"

The terse, gruff, no-nonsense command roots me to the spot.

I'm beyond frozen.

I'm petrified.

"Hands up!" Another gruff demand. "Now!"

"What are the cops saying?" asks Callie.

Finding my voice, I glance down at the cat, who sits at my feet, and whisper out of the side of my mouth, "They don't want me to move and I have to put my hands up, which I'm doing."

"Well, who called the cops?" asks Callie.

"I have no idea," I whisper. "I'm guessing one of the neighbors."

"Nosey busybodies," gripes Callie, hissing.

"Sophie ... is that you?"

Recognizing Officer Cuetee's voice, I'm filled with relief.

"Yes! It's me," I say, turning to face him.

His partner, a slim Palmchatter with lean muscles, frowns at me but doesn't lower his firearm. "You know this woman?"

Nodding, Officer Cuetee says, "And the cat, too."

"What did Officer Good-looking say?" asks Callie. "Are you in trouble? Are they going to arrest you?"

The partner's frown deepens as he cuts a glance toward Officer Cuetee. "You know the cat?"

Clearing his throat, Officer Cuetee motions for his partner to lower his weapon. "Sophie's harmless. As for the cat ... well, that's another story."

"Can I put my hands down now?" I ask.

"You sure she won't make a run for it?" asks the partner.

"Trust me, I'm not going to run away," I assure the partner. "I don't even like running. Just ask Officer Cuetee. Once, we went running, and—"

Callie swats a paw against my ankle.

"Owww ..." I looked down at her.

Staring up at me, she demands, "What are they saying? I already told you, sis, I'm not catching a charge for you, so—"

"I see what you mean about the cat," says the partner, taking a step back.

"Sophie, what are you doing here?" asks Officer Cuetee.

I clear my throat. "Well, um, you see—"

"What did he say?"

"What am I doing here?" I repeat, answering Callie's question. "Well, I, um ... am ... I mean, I was—"

"Tell him the truth," advises Callie. "You came here to question the hamster."

"I can't tell him that," I tell the cat.

"You can't tell who what?" asks the partner, frowning.

Mentally kicking myself, I try to remember not to talk to the cat while I'm talking to other humans. "I got a tip. A lead about ... an eyewitness to the crime ... and I came here to talk to the eyewitness."

"Okay, can we go now?" asks Callie.

Smiling at Officer Cuetee and his partner, I say, "Just a second ... I need a moment ... with ... my cat."

"Girl, what did I tell you about telling people that I'm your cat?" demands Callie.

Officer Cuetee and his partner look at each other, and then at me, their expressions a mix of amusement and frustration.

"There, there, kitty ... don't be scared ..." I say, bending over toward Callie.

"Don't be scared of what?" asks Callie, side-stepping backward. "And what did I tell you about calling me kitty? Girl—"

Without preamble, I reach for Callie and pick her up.

Which turns out to be a bad idea.

Immediately, the cat goes into psycho mode.

"Girl, you better put me down!" hisses Callie, swatting and kicking at the air as I hurry toward the dresser and put her down on it, praying she won't lunge at me.

"Will you calm down for a second?" I ask. "I need to talk to the police."

"You already talked to them," says Callie. "You told them why you were here. What more do they want?"

"There, there, don't be upset ..." I say the soothing words loud enough for Officer Cuetee and his partner to hear before I whisper to the cat, "They probably have more questions."

"More questions about what?"

"It's okay, it's okay ... " I look over my shoulder and give the officers another quick smile, which they don't return. Focusing on Callie, I say, "More questions about why we broke into the house."

"You can answer their questions if you want to," says the cat. "But I'm not talking without my lawyer present."

I gape at the feisty feline. "Your lawyer."

"See ya later, sis," says Callie, and then she leaps off the dresser onto the bed, and then off the bed and to the floor before taking off out of the room.

Exhaling a few muted curses under my breath, I turn to Officer Cuetee and his partner.

"Your cat just ran away," says the partner.

Rolling my eyes, I say, "Trust me, it's for the best."

Officer Cuetee sighs. "Okay, explain to us why you were here again. You said something about an eyewitness to a crime."

"I did?" I ask, wondering if I can feign ignorance.

"And you said you got a lead," says the partner. "A tip to come here and talk to the eyewitness."

"Yes, well ..." I start.

"Who gave you the tip?" asks Officer Cuetee.

"An anonymous caller," I say.

"And who's the eyewitness?" asks the partner.

I bite my lip. There's no way I can tell them the witness is a hamster, who happens to be missing.

Instead, I say, "I'm not sure ... that's why I came here ... to find out who the eyewitness is ... "

"You mean, that's why you broke into this house?" asks Officer Cuetee.

"I wouldn't say that I broke in," I say.

"What would you say that you did?"

"I would say that I can explain everything," I say, "but it will probably make more sense if I explain it to you over a steaming mug of hot tea."

Chapter 12

"Are you sure your source is going to show up?" I glance at Callie as I reach into my cross-body purse for a scrunchie to tie my unruly curls back.

Callie and I are at a local park near the pier. It's small, but pretty and picturesque with several palm tree-lined pathways, and benches surrounded by clusters of colorful hibiscus bushes.

The cat lounges next to me on the bench, lazily licking her fur as though she doesn't have a care in the world.

I, on the other hand, have several cares.

For one, my lunch break is almost over—I only get an hour—and I'm not going to get a chance to accomplish what I'd planned, which is visiting my favorite tea shop. While checking my social media feeds at work this morning, I made my last cup of mango and blood orange tea. Needless to say, it was very distressing. Mango and blood orange tea is sort of my world, so when I run out, I have to replenish forthwith.

And for two, Marty assigned me two stories, and he expects the first drafts of both on his desk by the end of the day. Luckily, the stories don't involve murder or mayhem, but I haven't even started writing. Marty will turn every shade of red, from rose to ruby, if I don't meet his deadline.

And for three ...

Hmmm. Well, I guess I only have two cares. But, still, those are huge cares. Especially the tea. And now, because of Callie, I won't have time to get a replacement box of mango and blood orange tea. Thirty minutes ago, I walked out to the *Palmchat Gazette* employee parking lot, and there was the feline, sitting on the hood of my JEEP.

"Well, hello, there stranger," I'd greeted her, not bothering to hide the sarcasm in my tone. "Long time, no see. Oh, wait, no. I have seen you recently. Last night, to be exact, running away from the scene of the crime, leaving me to deal with the cops!"

"Lose the attitude, sis," advised the cat. "I got a lead in the Tobacco Coast murder case. We gotta go."

I shook my head. "I'm not breaking into any more houses with you."

"We're not breaking into a house," the cat said. "We're going to talk to somebody who knows how to find the missing hamster."

Of course, I decided to follow the cat's lead. After all, the hamster can crack the Tobacco Coast murder case wide open. He knows who killed Cynthia Snowpearce. And after he gives me all the details, I plan to write an explosive story that will prove to Marty, once and hopefully for all, that I have "it."

Of course, that favorable outcome is contingent upon finding the hamster and getting his story, which is contingent on Callie's source showing up, which is starting to seem doubtful.

"Relax, sis," says the cat. "BeBe will be here."

Trying to temper my irritation, I ask, "And who is BeBe anyway?"

"I told you," says Callie. "BeBe has information about the missing hamster. She knows what happened to him. And how to find him."

"And you trust her information?"

"BeBe has all the tea," says the cat. "She's just as reliable as

Officer Good Looking. And speaking of him, I'm assuming he didn't arrest you."

"He probably should have," I say. "But he let me off with a warning."

The cat licks her left foot. "Girl, that's because he likes you."

"I don't know about that ..." A buzzing near my ear startles me for a moment. "I mean, I do think he likes me. But, I don't know if he likes me, likes me, you know?"

"Has he tried to shoot his shot, or not?"

"That's just it ..." I drape an arm over the back of the bench, and—

The buzzing makes me jump again. Glancing around, I wave a hand near my ear. Was that a bee?

"Anyway, I don't really know if he's shot his shot," I say. "I think he has, but—"

"Have you gone out on a date with him?"

"We've had dinner a few times. And we've met for tea, but—"

The droning buzz causes me to whip my head around, just in time to see the bumble bee hovering inches from my face.

"Oh, my God!" Swatting both hands near my face, I jump up from the bench.

Callie jumps to all fours, arching her back. "Girl, what is your problem?"

"There's a bee!" I tell her, whipping my head back and forth as I fan my hands in front of my nose, trying to shoo the bee away. "I don't want to get stung!"

"Girl, relax!" says Callie.

"How can I relax?" I sidestep to the left, and then to the right, but the bee insists on following me, buzzing around my head. "Get away from me bee!"

"Sophie, stop!" Callie calls to me.

But, I'm not going to stop. If I stop, the bee will sting me, and that's the last thing I need. An allergic reaction. Not that I'm allergic to bees, but …

"Leave me alone!" I shout, twirling around, running in a semi-circle, swatting at the bee, desperate to get away from the thing. "Go away!"

My efforts have the opposite effect on the bee, which seems determined, for some odd reason, to fly as close to my face as possible. Nevertheless, I'm determined not to get stung. Yelping, I karate chop my hands through the air trying to disorient the bee. When that doesn't work, I flap my arms like a chicken, which causes two little boys to giggle and point while their mother hurries them away from me. As a last resort, I windmill my arms, hoping—

"Girl, what are you doing?" Callie hisses, leaping from the bench toward me.

Screaming, I try to avoid the feline's lunge, but she sinks her claws onto my shirt. Off-kilter, I stumble back and slip on the grass, falling onto the waxy green blades.

"Sophie, relax, girl …" says the cat, placing a paw over my mouth.

I mumble a response about not being able to relax as I look around, trying to determine the location of the bee.

"You have to calm down," says Callie, carefully removing her paw. "You can't kill BeBe before she tells us how to find the hamster!"

"How could I kill BeBe?" I ask, confused.

"You were swatting at her."

"Swatting at her?" I ask, pushing myself up to a sitting position.

Callie bobs her head.

"Wait. Is Bebe—

"A bee," confirms Callie.

"Oh, my God!" I scramble to my feet, brushing dust and blades of grass from my skirt. "Why didn't you tell me BeBe is a bee?"

"Why didn't you ask?"

"Can't believe I almost killed her!" I groan. "Where is she now? She didn't fly away did she?"

"She's over on the bench waiting for us," says Callie. "Come on."

Moments later, I carefully sit on the bench.

"Please tell BeBe that I'm so very sorry," I tell the cat. "I didn't mean to try to kill her."

"Relax, sis," says Callie, jumping up onto the bench. "BeBe's used to it. Most humans are afraid of bees while bees are busy minding their business."

Alighting from the bench, the bee circles Callie's head.

Following the bee's movements, Callie says, "So what's the tea about the hamster? Where is he? What happened to him?"

The bee buzzes her answer, zipping and zooming between me and Callie.

"Are you serious?" says Callie to the bee. "Interesting."

The bee continues to buzz and fly around Callie.

"Well, that was probably for the best," says Callie.

"What was probably for the best?" I ask, anxious to know the fate of the hamster.

"What happened to the hamster was probably the best thing for him," says the cat.

Tempering my frustration, I ask, "What was the best thing that happened to the hamster?"

Callie says, "The cops took him to an animal shelter."

Chapter 13

The St. Mateo Furry Friends Center, an animal shelter near the marina, is housed in a weather-beaten, faded pink stone building that was once a court office centuries ago.

After BeBe the honeybee told me and Callie that the hamster had been removed from the scene of the crime and taken to an animal shelter, I decided to call Marty and tell him I had a lead on a possible eyewitness to Cynthia Snowpearce's murder.

Marty sounded suspicious, but encouraged my efforts and said, "Don't blow it, Sophia ... though I have a feeling you'll find some way to ... "

In the cool vestibule of the animal shelter, Callie and I are greeted by a receptionist.

"Oh, hello, there!" greets a plump, elderly woman with an expansive smile. "And who is this pretty little girl? Hi, there, cutie!"

"What is she saying?" demands Callie, wiggling in the crook of my arm.

"Stay still ..." I whisper out of the side of my mouth, then say to the receptionist, "Her name is Callie ..."

"Callie!" says the woman, clapping her hands in what can only be described as joyous delight. "What a pretty name for a pretty girl! Do you want some kibble, pretty girl?"

"What is she talking about?" Callie wants to know.

"Callie, the nice lady is going to give you some kibble," I say, as the receptionist turns and walks to a shelf behind the desk. "Isn't that nice?"

Hissing, Callie says, "Kibble? Girl, please. I never touch that stuff. Now, if she has tuna, I'll take that, but it must be fresh. I don't eat that canned stuff you humans mix with mayonnaise and spread on crackers."

"You know, I'm sorry ... " I say. "She already ate, so ... "

Returning to the desk, the receptionist says, "Oh, well, okay ... now, how can I help you? Are you here to adopt another animal? I know you're not here to give up this pretty girl."

"No, no ... " I say, allowing Callie to leap from my arms down to the floor. "Actually, I'm here about a hamster."

The woman frowns. "A ... hamster."

"Tell her that the cops brought him here after his owner was killed and we need to talk to him," instructs Callie.

Clearing my throat, I say, "I believe the police brought a hamster to this shelter a week ago."

"Oh, the hamster who was brought in by the police last week," repeats the jolly woman, smiling.

"Is the hamster still here?" I ask.

"Oh, I have no idea," she says. "I don't know anything about a hamster the police brought to the shelter."

Frowning, I say, "Oh. Well ..."

"But, maybe my coworker does," announces the woman as she picks up the desk phone. "Let me buzz her."

Several minutes later, the jolly woman's coworker joins us at the front counter.

She's thin with pale skin, dark red hair, and down turned mouth.

With an impatient sullenness, she crosses her arms over her chest and sneers at me. Her attitude is the exact opposite of her counterpart.

Clearing my throat, I say, "I'm inquiring about a hamster the police brought to the shelter a week ago."

"You're out of luck," says the sullen girl, with what seems to be a hint of a nasty smile. "He's already been adopted."

"Oh no ..." I say, disappointed.

"That is a shame," says the jolly woman, giving me a look of sympathy. "Did you have your heart set on taking that precious little baby home?"

Knowing that I can't reveal my intent to question the hamster, I shrug. "Um, yeah ... sort of ..."

"That's too bad," says Sullen Girl, though I doubt she feels any sympathy toward me. On the contrary, she seems happy that I'm upset.

"Um, you don't happen to know who adopted the hamster?" I ask.

Nodding, the Sullen Girl says, "I know exactly who adopted him."

Thinking that there might still be a chance to talk to the hamster, I ask, "Who's the lucky family?"

"I'm not telling you," says the Sullen Girl, giving me the half-smile, half-sneer.

"Oh, honey, I'm sorry, we can't tell you," says the jolly lady. "That information is private."

"I understand." I sigh. "Well, thanks for your time. Me and Callie will be on our way."

I glance down toward my ankle.

And frown.

Callie isn't there.

"What's the matter?" asks the jolly woman.

"Um ... " Worried, I glance around the reception lobby. "I don't know where my cat is ..."

"Oh my goodness!" cries the jolly woman. "How terrible! We have to find her!"

And we do.

Five minutes later, we locate her in the dog kennel, of all places.

Back in the JEEP, I turn to the cat. "Why were you in the dog kennel?"

"Well, I wasn't looking for a canine to adopt," says the cat, settling into the passenger seat. "I was helping you out."

I start the JEEP. "Helping me out?"

"Getting information about the hamster," says the cat, licking her fur.

"What kind of information about the hamster?" I ask, shifting the JEEP into drive before steering out of the parking lot. "Do the dogs know what happened to him? Did they tell you?"

"Of course, they told me," says Callie. "Dogs always snitch. That's why cops use them to sniff out drugs. Cats know things, but we keep those things to ourselves ... "

I shoot the cat a dubious look, then ask," So what happened to the hamster?"

"One of those mangy old strays was waiting to go through the intake process when the family was adopting the hamster," says the feline. "The dad gave his name as Roger West and the address was some house in Old Ocean."

Chapter 14

"So, before we talk to the new owners," I say, pulling the JEEP alongside the curb in front of the spacious bungalow. "We need to come up with a story."

The decision to head to the home of Roger West, the hamster's adoptive *pawrents*, was a no-brainer. After a quick public records search, executed on an app Marty told all of the reporters to download, Callie and I headed to Old Ocean.

Callie the Calico stares at me then turns her head to lick her neck. "What kind of story?"

"A cover story," I say, a sizzle of adrenaline shooting through me. "You know, we need to give the hamster's new owners a good reason why we're here."

"We're here to talk to the hamster."

"But we can't just tell them that," I say.

The cat licks her right hind leg. "Why not?"

"Because they might not let us talk to him," I say.

"Well, we are not going to be talking to him," clarifies the cat. "Only I can talk to him. You don't speak hamster."

"I know that," I tell her. "What I mean is … I can't just tell the owner, Hi, my name is Sophie Carter and this Calico cat, whose name is Callie, wants to question your foster hamster about the heinous murder of his owner, which he witnessed."

Callie stares at me with disdain. "Again ... why not?"

Exhaling my frustration, I say, "Because I'll look like a stark, raving, psycho if I tell the hamster's fosters that a cat wants to talk to him. They'll ask me how I know that and if I tell them, well the cat told me she needs to talk to him, they'll look at me like I'm crazy because, as I'm sure you know, every other human on the planet besides me knows that cats don't talk to people."

"Okay, sis, maybe you have a point," concedes the cat. "But you humans need to be a bit more open-minded. None of my animal friends thinks I'm crazy when they find out that you speak cat."

I frown at Callie. "I don't speak cat."

"Then how do I understand you?" asks Callie.

"Because you speak English," I say.

The feline bobs her head. "Right. I speak English to you. And you speak cat to me."

Tilting my head, I say, "Yeah, I get it. Your meows sound like English to me. And my English is translated into meows that you understand."

"The point is, sis, that we can understand each other," says the cat.

"But you can't understand any other humans, right?"

"Girl, we already established that," says the cat.

"But you don't know why I'm the only human you can understand."

"You're the only human I need to understand," the feline tells me.

"But, maybe ..."

The cat stares at me. "Maybe what?"

"Maybe you actually can understand other humans," I say. "I

mean, all the other animals you know can understand humans, right?"

Bobbing her head, the cat says, "They just can't talk to humans."

"That's why it's weird that you can't understand any other human except me," I say. "Maybe the selective amnesia has affected your ability to understand other humans."

"Maybe. Maybe not," says Callie. "Anyway, understanding you is quite enough. I'm not upset that I can't understand other humans. From what my friends tell me, most of you humans aren't saying anything that matters anyway."

"I guess you're right," I say, but I'm not so sure. Part of me still wonders how the cat and I could possibly be communicating. It doesn't make sense that we understand each other. There is no rational, logical explanation for a talking cat. And yet, Callie talks. Or, does she?

Shaking away the worrisome thoughts, I say, "Okay … about our story. Here's what I think we should say …"

Moments later, I'm standing on the porch, with Callie sitting quietly at my feet, knocking on Roger West's front door.

Minutes pass, but no one answers.

"Wonder if they're not home," I say, glancing back at the driveway, where a small compact car is parked.

"Try the doorbell, sis," suggests the cat.

Sheepish, and a tad embarrassed, I ring the bell and say, "That was going to be my next move."

"Girl, whatever …"

The door opens.

A thirtyish woman with short, wispy blonde hair and large brown eyes gives me a curious look. "Can I help you?"

"I certainly hope so," I begin. "My name is Sophie Carter, and recently my friend, Cynthia Snowpearce, passed away ... and she had a hamster who was taken by the police and placed in a shelter. The people at the shelter told me that you and your family adopted the hamster ..."

"Yes, we did adopt him," says the woman, her expression grave.

"Well, I want to thank you for doing that," I go on. "The hamster was very important to Cynthia so I'm glad he has a loving family, but ... um, my cat, Callie—"

"Girl, if you don't stop telling people that I'm your cat ... "

Ignoring the feline, I say, "Callie and the hamster were ... friends ... and she misses the hamster, so I was wondering if it wouldn't be too much trouble if Callie could spend a little time with the hamster? She's been a little depressed and not eating since she hasn't seen him—"

"You're laying it on a bit thick, sis," cautions the cat.

Clearing my throat, I say, "I certainly understand if you don't feel comfortable—"

"No, no, no ..." The woman stops me, giving me a bittersweet smile. "I wouldn't mind at all. I think it's sweet that the cat and the hamster are friends."

"Oh, so do I ..." I say, clapping my hands in delight, buoyed at the thought of discovering the person who killed Cynthia Snowpearce, excited by the prospect of writing an exclusive, propulsive article. Already, I can see myself on Good Morning Caribbean, telling my story to millions of viewers, and—

"But, I'm afraid I can't help you."

Confused, I stare at the woman. "Huh? I mean, what? No, I mean ... um, I thought you said you wouldn't mind."

"I wouldn't mind the cat and the hamster spending time

together," says the woman, smiling down at Callie before focusing on me again. "But we don't have the hamster anymore."

Crushed, I feel my hopes deflating. "I don't understand."

Shaking her head, the woman says, "It was such a shame, actually. My husband Roger and I got the hamster for our little girl, and she did love it, but … turned out she was allergic to the hamster."

"Oh, no …" I say. "So … did you take him back to the shelter?"

"Oh, no …" The woman smiles, eyes watery with unshed tears. "As a family, we made the painful decision to let him go, so he can be …"

"You let him go … so he can be?" I ask, confused.

"We set him free into the wild," says the woman, "where God intended for him to be …"

Chapter 15

"I need your opinion about something," I begin, glancing at Clark over the rim of my teacup.

It's a few minutes after eight in the morning. Clark and I will be attending Marty's daily morning meeting at nine, but we have an hour to kill, so we're killing it in the breakroom. Of course, I should be fact-checking articles and Clark should be doing whatever he does as a staff photographer, but I can't resist blood orange and rosewater tea and he's a coffee fiend, so here we are …

Two days have passed since Callie and I came up empty in our valiant quest to find the hamster. Since then, Callie's been asking her furry friends about where he might be, but the cat has not had much luck.

"Okay …" says Clark, glancing at me over the rim of his coffee mug.

"You think a pet hamster can survive in the jungle?" I ask.

Shaking his head, Clark says, "I doubt it. From what I know, pet hamsters were raised to be pets and probably wouldn't know how to survive in the wild and most likely wouldn't last very long and would probably be eaten by a jungle predator."

Disappointed, I sigh. "Yeah, that's what Callie thinks, too …"

When I relayed my conversation with Roger West's wife to the feline, she asked, "When did they release the hamster into the wild?"

"You know, I didn't ask," I'd admitted. "I'm assuming a few days ago, maybe."

The cat gave me a look. "Well, he's dead by now."

"Oh, Callie, don't say that," I admonished.

"Girl, be realistic," said the cat. "That was a house hamster. A pet. He probably got swallowed by a snake before the sun went down."

"But, we don't know that for sure," I said. "Maybe the hamster drew on some inner strength, grit, or tenacity and he's finding a way to stay alive."

"Strength, grit, and tenacity," said the cat. "Don't those words mean the same thing, sis?"

Sheepish, and a bit embarrassed, I said, "The point is … the hamster may be dead. Or, he may not be dead. But, we need to find out, don't you think?"

Callie did not think determining the fate of the hamster was imperative, as she considers his death a forgone conclusion, but considering I need the hamster to reveal Cynthia Snowpearce's killer, the feisty feline agreed to see what she could find out.

"But, I'm not making any promises, sis," she warned.

Clark says, "Callie thinks that too?"

Focusing on his dreamy green-gray eyes, which may actually be gray-green, I'm not entirely sure, I say, "Huh?"

"You said Callie thinks so, too," repeats Clark. "Callie as in … your cat."

Clearing my throat, I stare at Clark, trying to figure out how to answer him and wondering why I keep making the mistake of referring to Callie as though she's a friend and not a feisty feline.

"Um, I don't have a cat," I say, then take another quick sip of tea.

Giving me a sneaky smile, Clark asks, "Why are you wondering if a pet hamster can survive in the jungle? You plan on releasing one into the wild?"

"Oh, no, no," I insist. "I just hope the hamster will survive."

"I'm confused," says Clark. "What hamster are you talking about and why do you hope he'll survive?"

"The hamster belonged to Cynthia Snowpearce," I say. "After she was murdered, the cops took the hamster to a shelter, where he was adopted, but the family had to release him into the jungle because their little girl was allergic to him. So ... "

"You're worried about the hamster," says Clark, taking another sip of coffee.

Nodding, I say, "He's already experienced so much trauma and then to be left in the jungle to fend for himself. He must be in a complete and total panic by now."

"What trauma did the hamster experience?" asks Clark. "Was he abused or neglected?"

"No, I don't think so," I say. "But, he did witness Cynthia's murder."

Clark frowns. "How do you know that?"

I clear my throat. "Well, I got an anonymous tip."

"Someone gave you an anonymous tip about the hamster witnessing Cynthia's murder?" The voice, which belongs to Candace, the *Palmchat Gazette* receptionist-slash-Assignments Editor, startles me.

Gasping, I glance over my shoulder.

Candace leans against the counter in front of the coffee bar, swigging from a bottle of water.

"Candace!" I exclaim. "I didn't see you there."

"Because your back was to me," says Candace. "I've been standing here for about fifteen minutes."

"Actually seventeen minutes," says Clark, tapping the face of his watch.

Candace shrugs. "Fifteen. Seventeen. What's the difference?"

"Two," I say.

"Impressive," announces Candace, raising the water bottle toward me. "I wouldn't have guessed that you would be able to do subtraction in your head."

Tilting my head, I stare at the receptionist. Of course, I wonder why she didn't think I could subtract in my head, but I wonder a lot of things about Candace.

"Anyway, back to the anonymous tip about the hamster witnessing the murder," says Candace. "How did the anonymous tipster know that?"

"I have no clue," I say, wondering if I should ask Callie how the gossipy bird got her information.

"Well, that's not surprising," says Candace, finishing her water.

"What's not surprising?" I ask.

"You never have a clue," says Candace, smiling as she tosses the empty bottle into a trash bin beneath the sink. "That's why, one day, Marty will be successful in his quest to fire you."

I stare at Candace, flabbergasted by her flippant attitude toward my employment.

"Sophie's not going to be fired," says Clark.

"Well, we don't know that," declares Candace. "But, I know someone who could find out."

"Who?" I ask.

"The tentacle reader down at the beach," says Candace.

"Wait," I say, confused. "What?"

Clark frowns. "You want Sophie to go to a jellyfish fortune teller?"

"I heard she's very accurate," says Candace. "Especially when she's reading a Portuguese Man-O-War. After our meeting, you should head down there before the line gets too long."

Minutes after Candace departs the kitchen, I look at Clark. "You know, she's a very strange goat."

"Definitely," agrees Clark. "But, back to Cynthia Snowpearce. I meant to tell you that I was doing a little more research into her, and—"

"Why were you researching Cynthia Snowpearce?" I ask, slightly suspicious. "You're not trying to poach my story, are you?"

"Poach your story?" Clark laughs. "Do I look like an investigative journalist?"

Tilting my head to the right, I stare at Clark and squint just a tad. Then a tilt my head to the left.

"What are you doing?" asks Clark.

"I'm trying to see if you look like an investigative journalist?"

Rolling his eyes, Clark says, "I didn't expect you to answer me."

"Well ..." I shrug. "Just so you know, when I tilt my head to the left, you kind of do."

Clark exhales. "I was doing research to help you with your investigation. I know how hard Marty comes down on you."

"Aw ..." I smile. "That's very sweet of you."

Clark shrugs, but I see a hint of a blush creeping across his cheeks.

"So ... you have a lead?" I ask, hoping not to embarrass him further.

"I came across an article that listed one of Cynthia Snowpearce's accomplices," says Clark. "I wrote his name down and looked him up. He's got a criminal record. And you'll never guess what he was arrested for ..."

"Oh, I love a guessing game," I confess. "Kidnapping?"

"Nope."

"Money laundering?"

"No."

"Public intoxication?"

"Negative."

"Insurance fraud?"

Shaking his head, Clark says, "Fencing stolen jewelry."

"Wow, you were right," I say. "I never would have guessed that, even though it makes sense. Cynthia Snowpearce was a jewel thief. She would need a fence."

"A fence who might have killed her," suggests Clark.

"You could be right," I agree.

"We should find out," says Clark. "The fence lives here in St. Mateo. After the staff meeting, we should pay him a visit …"

Chapter 16

"All of a sudden, I'm not so sure that this was the best idea," I confess as I park the JEEP alongside a shallow ditch in front of the fence's house in the Hilaire-Honoréneighborhood, located on the east side of the island.

Painted pink with white trim, the residence is complimented by a lemon tree in the small front yard, which has a crushed oyster driveway and a paver stone pathway leading to the front door. It appears to be one of the nicer houses in the neighborhood, which is not known for its stunning mansions, but for its rows of dilapidated homes, which seem abandoned even when they're occupied.

After the staff meeting, which wasn't too horrific even though Marty shouted and turned seventeen shades of purple during his tirade, Clark and I did a public records search on the fence: Horace J. Feather VI.

Sitting in the passenger seat of my JEEP, Clark turns his head toward me. "Okay, maybe it's not the best idea, but it's a good idea. Why the cold feet?"

Shifting the JEEP into park, but keeping the vehicle running, I twist in my seat toward Clark. "As we were driving over here, I was thinking ..."

"When were you thinking?" questions Clark, with a sly smirk. "You've been singing along to the latest CoCo album since the time we left the *Palmchat Gazette* until the moment we got here."

Folding my arms, I give Clark a look. "I wasn't singing the whole time."

"Okay, so, maybe not the whole time," Clark says. "You didn't sing the high notes or the whistle tones."

Laughing at his not-so-subtle dig, I give him a playful punch in his rock-solid bicep. "For your information, I'm an alto, so, no ... I don't do whistle notes, but ... "

"But tell me what you were thinking?" asks Clark. "You don't think we should question the fence?"

"I'm just not sure what questions to ask," I confide, biting my lower lip. "How do I get him to spill the tea without realizing that he's spilling piping, hot tea, you know?"

Rubbing the cleft in his chin, Clark says, "The way I see it, we can be direct ... or indirect."

"Okay ..." I nod, then say, "I'm not sure I'm following you."

"Well, we could just come out and ask the fence if he killed Cynthia Snowpearce."

"Obviously, he'll say no, he didn't kill her."

"Unless he's honest and admits to strangling her," counters Clark.

"Which I doubt he'll do," I say.

"But suppose he doesn't like the fact that he killed Cynthia," says Clark. "I mean, he's a fence, a criminal, but he doesn't think of himself as a murderer. Cynthia's death might have been weighing on his conscience for some time. Might be a heavy burden, one that he's been looking to unload."

I give Clark a look. "Yeah, maybe but I still don't think he's gonna confess to us."

"You're probably right," says Clark, with a sigh. "I was just thinking that if he is looking to confess, we could use a direct method of questioning, which is a lot less complicated than an indirect method of questioning, and save ourselves the time and trouble of trying to be sly and cunning."

Nodding, I say, "I wish it could be that easy, too."

"If wishes were goats, right?" says Clark, grinning as he starts the popular Palmchatter saying.

"Then we'd all have nice lawns," I say, completing the saying, which basically boils down to this: if wishing could make things happen, then everyone could afford a goat to eat the grass. Now, technically, I don't officially understand the logic behind this saying, but it's an old Palmchat proverb, so I don't question it.

"I'm guessing we'll have to be indirect," says Clark, opening his door.

"I'm guessing you're right," I say, exiting the JEEP.

The air is stagnant due to a low cloud deck, blocking the sun and the sea breeze. As we walk to the door, I reach into my cross-body purse for a scrunchie. With this humidity, what I need is my anti-frizz serum, but tying my wild curls back will have to suffice.

At the door, Clark rings the bell.

A sizzle of excitement tinged with fear and anticipation shoots down my spine.

A minute, or so passes but no one opens the door.

"Maybe he's not home," I suggest, feeling a little letdown. "Or, sleeping. Or, looking at us from a window and deciding not to answer the door because he doesn't know us and thinks we're trying to sell him something, like goat chops."

"We should have called first," says Clark, ringing the doorbell again, and then using his fist to bang on the wood.

Another minute, or so passes and no one opens the door.

Exhaling, Clark says, "I think this might have been a wasted trip—"

"You looking for Horace?" calls out a raspy disembodied voice.

I glance at Clark, who stares at me.

"Over here!"

"Over ... where?" I call out.

The voice says, "Next door ..."

Shrugging, I follow Clark off the porch and across the lawn to the house to the right of Horace's place. On the porch of the aqua-colored house, a wizened old woman sits in a rocking chair. She wears a neon green muumuu that reminds me of a highlighter and a matching headscarf.

"I heard you knocking," says the old woman. "You need Horace?"

Nodding, I say, "Yes. Do you know where to find—"

"Horace probably in the backyard," says the old woman. "You can go on back there."

Minutes later, in the backyard, Clark and I find a woman working on an old car. She wears dirty overalls and her face, which is the color of wet sand and suggests mixed ancestry, is smudged and stained with grease. Her spiral curls are piled in a messy bun on top of her head.

"Um ... we're looking for Horace ..." I say.

The woman maneuvers from beneath the opened hood and faces us. "Do I know you?"

"No, I don't think so," I tell her, focusing on her features, trying to remember if I've seen her before. "But, I suppose it's possible that I don't recall—"

"No, we've never met," interjects Clark, before introducing himself. "And this is my friend, Sophie Carter. We both work at the *Palmchat Gazette* and we'd like to ask Horace some questions about a story we're working on if he can spare a few minutes."

"Is Horace home?" I ask.

The woman frowns. "I'm Horace."

"You're Horace?" asks Clark, the confusion in his voice matching my shock. "Horace J. Feather VI?"

Rolling her eyes, Horace says, "Let me guess. Not what you were expecting, right? Dude, if I had a dollar for every time someone has said, 'you're Horace' …"

"You'd have a million dollars," I finish.

Wiping her hands on her overalls, Horace shakes her head. "No, not that much. Just a hundred bucks, or so."

Clark shakes his head. "Are you sure you're Horace? The Horace J. Feather VI we're looking for is definitely a *he*."

"People always think I'm a he," she says. "All my public records are messed up because when I fill out forms, I list myself as a *she*, which I most definitely am, but some clerk will see my name and decide that I have to be a *he*. It's a nightmare. My mom and grandma and aunts and cousins go through the same thing."

"Your mom and grandma and aunts and cousins are named Horace, too?" I ask.

"Only the girl cousins are named Horace," she clarifies. "But, yeah. Anyway, how can I help you?"

"Well, as I said, we came to talk to you," I start.

"About what?"

"I'm working on a story about the murder of Cynthia Snowpearce," I begin. "And—"

"Okay, before you go any further," says Horace, holding up a hand to stop me. "I'll tell you what I told that grumpy, good-looking detective."

"François?" I guess.

"First of all," says Horace, "I didn't kill Cynthia."

"Are you sure about that?" asks Clark, giving Horace a shrewd look.

Sneering, Horace says, "I think I would know if I had killed someone. I didn't kill Cynthia. I didn't have a reason to."

"You fence stolen goods," says Clark. "Maybe Cynthia tried to betray you and you killed her because she refused to pay you your cut."

"Okay, second of all, like I told the detective," says Horace, "I don't fence anymore. I'm not about that life. I fix cars now. Which is what I told Cynthia and that pip squeak she came here with."

"Pip squeak?" Asks Clark.

Horace rolls her eyes. "Some gangly, pimple-faced kid. Smelly jerk wearing a suit ten times too big for him."

"A suit ten times too big for him," I repeat, finding the detail familiar, for some reason.

Clark asks, "What did Cynthia say when you told her you were no longer a fence?"

"Just shrugged and said she'd find someone else," says Horace.

"And did she?" I ask.

"Not that I know," says Horace. "Like I said, I'm not in that life anymore. So people don't talk to me and I don't talk to them, you know?"

"You have any idea who might have killed Cynthia?" asks Clark.

"Cynthia wasn't the type to make enemies," says Horace. "She was into making connections. But, again, like I told the cops—they asked me the same question—I have no idea."

"Let me ask you this," I say. "What did Cynthia want you to fence?"

"Diamonds," says Horace. "What else? Diamond theft was her specialty."

Chapter 17

Deep in thought, I walk slowly across the employee parking lot at the end of the workday.

Since Clark and I returned to the *Palmchat Gazette* several hours ago—after a stop for lunch—I've been pondering something Horace told us about the gangly pip squeak who showed up with Cynthia Snowpearce when the jewel thief inquired about fencing diamonds.

Smelly jerk ... wearing a suit ten times too big for him.

I've been thinking about why that detail seems so familiar, and I'm happy to report I finally figured it out. I'm equally happy to announce that figuring it out only took two cups of tea. Normally, it takes me three cups of tea to connect the dots between the various and sundry ideas and speculation floating in my head.

Anyway, Horace's description of Cynthia Snowpearce's companion is nearly the same way Mr. Beauchamp described the guy who, along with the beautiful blonde, robbed his store.

He wore an expensive suit, I could tell, but it hung off his frame ... he smelled like sour goat milk.

Of course, I couldn't help but conclude that Mr. Beauchamp and Horace were talking about the same guy. He was, according to Mr.

Beauchamp a troll. Or a toad. And Horace said he was a pip squeak. So, then I couldn't help but think that the beautiful woman who pulled the gun on Beauchamp was Cynthia Snowpearce, the diamond thief. Now, I'm wondering about the identity of the troll/toad pip squeak who smelled like sour goat milk. Who is he? Could he have killed Cynthia? Maybe Cynthia tried to double-cross him? Or maybe she tried to abscond with all the diamonds, leaving the troll/toad pip squeak with nothing to show for his crimes?

Exhaling, I glance up at the late afternoon St. Mateo sky, staring at the wispy cotton candy pink and baby blue clouds. I need to find the troll/toad pip squeak who smelled like sour goat milk. But how?

At my JEEP, I glance at the hood.

Callie the Calico is not there. A pang of longing assails me. I'd grown used to seeing the feisty feline lounging on my car. I can't help but wonder where she is, and what she's up to. I'm assuming she's here or there, somewhere being independent and sassy.

Opening the driver's door, I glance at the Seagrape tree I rescued Callie from. How did she get tangled in the tree? So weird. I focus on the medium-sized tree. Doesn't appear that an animal could have gotten trapped between the twisting limbs. An animal could have climbed on the branches, but …

The cat would have had to, on purpose, get herself stuck in the tree. But why would Callie do that? And if Callie did trap herself in the tree—which, again, I feel is highly unlikely—then only she could tell me why she did that. But of course, Callie can't tell me because she doesn't remember …

I have selective catnesia.

Callie has a past she doesn't remember. I've promised to help her find out who she is, where she came from, and whether, or not, she already has a human. The idea always gives me bittersweet feelings, but if there's someone out there looking for Callie, I owe it to the cat, and the human, to find out.

Question is, how do I find out?

Biting my lower lip, I climb into the JEEP, close the door, and start the ignition. Backing out of the parking space, I check the rearview mirror. While doing so, the building across the street comes into view, and I notice something on the left corner of the stucco and brick two-story structure.

Is that … ?

I pull the JEEP back into the parking slot, cut the engine, and jump out.

On the building across the street, I notice a CCTV camera mounted in the brick. I take a few steps forward. The camera appears to be positioned in the direction of the Seagrape tree.

At once, something I never imagined occurs to me …

Maybe Callie didn't accidentally get stuck in the tree.

What if she was intentionally put there?

Chapter 18

"You were right," I say, smiling at Officer Cuetee after I take a generous sip of the tea. "Blackberry, honeysuckle, and pineapple is a wonderful flavor combination."

Giving me a teasing wink, the handsome beat cop says, "I thought you would like it."

"And the star fruit glazed donut holes are the perfect complement," I say, popping one into my mouth.

Officer Cuetee and I are at Too-a-Tea, a cute, quaint beach front tea cafe with colorful tropical décor where we scored a wooden bistro table on the deck. Before us, the Caribbean Sea stretches for miles, sparkling in the afternoon sunshine.

"So, I didn't just invite you to lunch because I wanted you to try this tea," says Officer Cuetee.

Curious, I ask, "There's another reason?"

"I wanted you to know that there's been some movement in the Cynthia Snowpearce murder investigation," he says. "Detective François arrested the killer."

"Are you serious?"

Officer Cuetee takes another sip of tea. "The suspect is William Peters."

"William Peters?" I ask. "Why does that name seem familiar? Wait. Does William Peters also go by the name Willie Peters?"

Nodding, Officer Cuetee says, "He and Cynthia Snowpearce were in a romantic relationship."

"One of Cynthia's neighbors suspected that Willie Peters had killed her," I say. "I should have followed up on that lead instead of trying to find that hamster, which turned out to be a waste of time."

"Wait. What?" Officer Cuetee puts his cup of tea down. "Why were you trying to find a hamster?"

"Oh, well, um, you see ..." I clear my throat, kicking myself for mentioning the hamster. "Cynthia Snowpearce had a hamster and ..."

"And ...?"

"And I was worried about the hamster," I say, reaching for another donut hold to put into my mouth.

"Why?"

Chewing slowly, I hold up a hand, indicating that I want Officer Cuetee to wait until I swallow the donut hole, which is, after all, proper etiquette. But truthfully, I'm trying to think of a reason why I would be worried about a dead woman's hamster. And then, just when I can't chew anymore or I'd basically be grinding my teeth, it hits me. I can give Officer Cuetee the same story I gave Roger West's wife about Callie and the hamster being friends.

After I explain that the feline and the little rodent are best buds, Officer Cuetee gives me an odd look.

Worried, I ask, "What?"

"How do you know the cat and the hamster are friends?"

"How do I know they're friends?" I parrot. I'm at a lost at how to answer the question and wish he'd just take my word like Roger West's wife did.

"I mean, she's not your cat, right?"

I clear my throat, and say, "No, you're right, she's not my cat and she will be the first one to tell you that."

"The cat will be the first one to tell me that she's not your cat?"

I clear my throat again. "Oh, no, I just meant ... the cat hangs around me a lot and once I saw her with the hamster and they seemed to be ... friendly toward each other ..."

Nodding, Officer Cuetee takes a sip of tea. "Interesting."

I hate lying to him, especially when I have a sinking suspicion that he doesn't believe me. "Right. So. Um, what's the evidence against Willie Peters?"

Officer Cuetee says, "The crime scene techs found a purple and neon green tie that belonged to Willie Peters with Cynthia's DNA on it. The tie was stuffed in a trash can behind the house. When they tested it, they recovered DNA from both Cynthia Snowpearce and William Peters.

"Additionally, the forensic pathologist found very thin, almost microscopic purple and neon green threads beneath Cynthia's fingernails, which he determined were there because she was probably fighting the killer, trying to claw the tie from her neck as he strangled her."

"Gruesome," I whisper, placing a hand against my neck as I try not to think of how helpless and terrified Cynthia Snowpearce must have felt with that tie around her throat, choking the life from her.

"Detective François confronted Willie Peters about the tie," says Officer Cuetee. "He admitted that it belonged to him. What he didn't admit to, obviously, was killing Cynthia."

"But he must have," I say. "The evidence against him is compelling."

"To hear him tell it, he has no idea how his tie ended up around Cynthia's neck," says Officer Cuetee. "He says he had no reason to kill Cynthia. He loved her. But Detective François thinks money was the motive for murder… "

"Money?"

"Actually, the money Cynthia and William planned to get from the sale of stolen diamonds," says Officer Cuetee.

Chapter 19

My desk phone rings as I'm powering down my computer and getting ready to leave.

It's been a long, taxing, tiring day but at least I had apricot, peach, and vanilla-flavored tea to help me get through it.

This morning, Marty assigned me to the police blotter, which he did because he said there was no way I could mess it up. Basically, I went to the police department's website to get details about the arrests that occurred last week and called the police department to ask for status updates.

The phone continues to ring. I make a face at it. I'm exhausted. All I want to do is go home, make myself a cup of mint and lavender tea, which is perfect for relaxing, and watch the sunset from my patio.

But, suppose the caller has a tip. And what if it's a real tip and not just some troll telling me to use an umbrella when it's raining? What if the caller has a compelling, interesting story that I need to investigate?

I grab the phone receiver and say, "*Palmchat Gazette*, this is Sophie Carter …"

"Hello, Ms. Carter, this is Bev!" announces a jolly, ebullient female voice.

"Bev ...?" I echo, wondering if I'm supposed to know her.

"From the Furry Friends Animal Shelter," says Bev. "You came in the other day with your pretty Calico cat."

"Oh, yes," I say, remembering. "I was asking about the hamster."

"I'm so sorry that didn't work out for you."

"Me, too," I say, plopping down in my swivel chair. "So ... how can I help you?"

"Well, after you and that lovely little girl of yours left," begins Bev, "I couldn't stop thinking about her."

"Really?" I ask, confused and curious. "Why not?"

"Because she seemed so familiar to me and I realized that I know her," says Bev.

"You know Callie?" I ask, dubious. "How?"

"Well, last year, when I was working at an animal shelter in St. Felipe," begins Bev, "we were informed about some kittens who were in really bad shape. They were scrounging and foraging for food in an old, abandoned sugar mill. Your Callie was one of those kittens."

"What?" I'm shocked. "Are you sure?"

"I am positive," says Bev. "The poor thing was in such bad shape. Her nose was clogged up, due to cat flu, and she could barely see because she had so much eye crust."

"Oh no," I say, immediately saddened for Callie.

"So, we set humane traps and eventually Callie made her way into the trap," says Bev. "She was so tiny and skittish but she crawled onto my lap. She was very emaciated, and I had to syringe-feed her. Callie responded wonderfully with food in her stomach and a warm, comfortable place to rest. All the kittens recovered."

"All the kittens," I say.

"Callie's siblings," says Bev. "There were five little babies. Anyway, soon Callie was able to eat from a bowl and she was breathing much easier and sleeping soundly with her brothers and sisters. Soon after, they all found their loving, forever homes! However, I guess I wasn't on duty when you adopted Callie because I don't remember you, but—"

"Bev, I didn't adopt Callie," I say. "I found her tangled in a Seagrape tree and I rescued her."

"Trapped in a tree!" Bev gasps. "Oh, my word!"

"I'm actually trying to find her owner," I say. "So what you've told me is great because now I can call the shelter in St. Felipe and find out who adopted her."

"Oh, how wonderful!" says Bev. "I'll give you the number of the shelter. When you call, ask for Gloria. Although, I'm not sure if she's still there because I haven't talked to anyone from the St. Felipe shelter in months."

After scrawling the number on a sticky note, I say, "Well, thanks so much for the information, Bev. I'm really anxious to find out who Callie belongs to."

"And I'm sure they're going to be thrilled to have her in their lives again," says Bev.

Minutes later, I end the call with Bev. Staring at the number of the St. Felipe shelter, I struggle to fight the disappointment threatening to overwhelm me. I feel bittersweet about Bev's information. On the one hand, I promised Callie I would help her find out more about her past so she could be reunited with her real human. But, still, I don't like the idea of turning Callie over to her family, even though she's not my cat.

Sighing, I stand and affix the sticky note to the small white board on the wall behind my computer.

I'll call the shelter tomorrow. And I'll make sure I have apple cinnamon and chamomile tea, which will give me the courage to do what I know is the right thing. Maybe not for me, but for Callie.

Moments later, as I walk across the employee parking lot to my car, I spot the cat sitting on the hood of my JEEP. As I wave at her, I decide that I'll keep Bev's information to myself, for now. Before I tell Callie about her rough start as an abandoned kitten scrounging for food, I want to call the shelter and learn the identity of her *pawrents*. It's occurred to me that reuniting Callie with her owner might not be so simple. After all, the feisty feline has selective catnesia. She might not remember her owner. Or what if the owner gave up looking for her and got another pet and no longer wants Callie? I don't know. It's a potentially delicate situation. I want to make the right decisions for all parties involved.

"Well, sis, I haven't had any luck finding the hamster," says Callie, after I greet her. "No one has seen him. I hate to say this, but I think he's dead."

"You're probably right," I agree, fighting the urge to reach out and scratch the feline behind her ear. "But it doesn't matter anymore."

"Why not?"

"Because the cops arrested a suspect," I tell her, leaning against the car. "Cynthia Snowpearce's boyfriend killed her. His name is Willie Peters."

The cat looks at me with her piercing green eyes. "Sis, I hate to tell you this, but finding the hamster alive is more important than ever."

Perplexed, I ask, "Why do you say that?"

"Because," says Callie. "The word on the curb is that the cops arrested the wrong guy."

Chapter 20

"I didn't kill Cynthia," says Willie Peters, staring at me with large, frightened eyes through the thick plastic glass of a visitor's booth at the St. Mateo City Jail.

This morning when I arrived at work, while I was having pineapple turmeric ginger tea and sugared lemon donut holes, Marty stopped by my cubicle to say, "I've arranged a jailhouse interview for you with the suspect in the Cynthia Snowpearce murder. Get down there and get the details."

"Details," I said. "I'll get them."

"You'd better, Sophia," warned Marty, scowling. "You're still on probation."

"Right," I mumbled, wishing he hadn't reminded me.

Clearing my throat, I say into the phone, "Well, the cops think you do."

"The cops are wrong about me," says Willie Peters.

Although he's slight and gangly with thin shoulders and a gaunt face, I don't think he looks like a troll or a toad. I'm not sure what a pip squeak looks like, so Horace might have been correct in her assessment.

"Cynthia's DNA was on a neon green and purple tie that belonged to you," I say, remembering what Officer Cuetee told me. "The police believe it's the same tie you used to strangle her."

"Should have gotten rid of that ridiculous tie," grumbles Willie Peters. "I never liked it. Cynthia bought it for me. It didn't even match any of my other clothes. Anyway, like I told the cops, I can explain how her DNA got on my tie."

"How?" I ask.

"Look, normally, I'm not a suit and tie kinda guy," says Willie. "I mean, I never learned how to tie a tie. So Cynthia had to show me. And she did so by putting the tie on herself, around her neck. That's how her DNA got on my tie."

Willie's explanation doesn't sound completely implausible, but I'm still not sure I believe him. Well, I do believe he probably didn't know how to tie a tie. He's sort of grungy and grimy. More likely to be found in an old, faded T-shirt and dingy jeans that haven't been washed in a while.

"And, like I told the detective, I didn't want Cynthia dead," insists Willie. "I loved her. I still do."

Willie's large brown eyes are watery. He seems sincere. Maybe he was in love with Cynthia Snowpearce. Or, maybe he's got bad allergies. The jail is sort of dank and humid. Stuffy and moldy.

"When I found her dead, I was devastated," says Willie.

"You found Cynthia's dead body?"

Nodding, Willie says, "And I was the one who called the cops."

"But you didn't stick around to give the cops a statement," I point out.

"I know I should have," says Willie, shaking his head. "I probably wouldn't be in this mess. But I panicked. Assumed the cops would arrest me for killing Cynthia which I did not do!"

"Detective François thinks you killed Cynthia because she was going to cheat you out of your cut of the money from the sale of the diamonds the two of you stole," I say.

Looking away, Willie says, "Like I told that detective, I don't know nothing about no stolen diamonds."

"So you're denying that you and Cynthia robbed Beauchamp & Daughters?" I ask.

"I'm not saying anything about stolen diamonds," says Willie, looking everywhere but directly at me as he scratches behind his left ear. "Not without my lawyer present. And maybe not even then."

"Okay, what do you have to say about this," I began. "If you didn't kill Cynthia, then who did? You have any ideas?"

Willie glares at me. "Yeah, I got ideas. One big idea, as a matter of fact."

"Would you like to tell me about that big idea?"

Shaking his head, Willie says, "Can't talk in here. Walls have ears. Eyes, too."

Assuming he's referring to the CCTV cameras mounted in the upper corners of the visitor's room, I say, "When are you getting out? Have you had a bail hearing?"

"Yesterday," he says. "Not that it mattered. I don't have the money to make bail."

"Which means you'll have to stay behind bars until your trial," I say.

"Right," agrees Willie. "Unless ..."

"Unless ...?"

"Unless somebody bails me out," says Willie, his left eye twitching slightly as he stares at me.

"Who would do that?" I ask. "Friends? Family?"

"Or someone who wants to know more about my big idea," says Willie.

At once, I get it.

"You mean ... me?"

"You get me out of here," says Willie. "And we can talk about my big idea. What do you say?"

Chapter 21

"I don't know, Sophia," says Marty, crushing his stress ball between his palms as he paces around his office.

Sitting in the chair in front of his desk, I twist in my seat to keep him in sight as he walks behind me. "What don't you know?"

"I'm not sure I like this idea of paying some homicidal psycho's bail," says Marty.

"But it's not a bad idea," I say, as Marty stomps in front of me. "And it's not like we'd be paying his bail out of the goodness of our hearts, or anything like that. We'd be getting information. An exclusive. It would be like quid pro quo."

Marty exhales as he makes another circle around the perimeter of his office. "Or maybe highway robbery."

"It'll be a fair exchange," I say, hoping to convince him.

An hour ago, after returning to the *Palmchat Gazette,* I made a beeline for Marty's office to present Willie Peters' proposal to him. But, Marty wasn't in his office. According to Candace, he was at lunch with an accounting representative. So, I had to wait for him to return, which I did, on pins and needles.

When Marty got back to the office, he wasn't in the mood to talk with me. Lunch hadn't gone well. Candace didn't have all the details, but Marty had asked her to get him an antiacid.

Even with his stomach feeling better, Marty still didn't seem interested in Willie's proposal, but I was determined to change his mind. And I'm still determined. I'm just hoping my tenacity won't be in vain.

"You sure this Willie Peters guy is going to tell you who killed Cynthia Snowpearce?" asks Marty, halting his pacing to give me a shrew glare.

I resist the urge to gulp and try to give him an enthusiastic and confident nod. "I am positive that he knows who really killed Cynthia."

Marty walks behind his desk and drops down into the leather chair, which of course, groans and creaks in protest. "So ... you don't think Willie killed Cynthia?"

"No, I don't," I say.

"Why not?" asks Marty, stroking the brittle stubble on his chin. "The evidence against Peters is solid. The murder weapon—that neon green and purple tie—belonged to him. He didn't deny that. He doesn't have an alibi for the night of the murder. Cynthia Snowpearce's neighbor told you that Willie threatened Cynthia. And let's not forget that Willie and Cynthia robbed Beauchamp & Daughters."

"I haven't forgotten that," I say.

"There's no honor among thieves, Sophia," says Marty. "Cynthia might have tried to cheat Willie. That's a compelling motive for murder."

"I know that, but ..."

"But?" prompts Marty.

The truth is not something I can share with Marty. Following my conversation with Willie, I wasn't convinced of his innocence. Or the validity of his supposed big idea. But when I went home that afternoon, I made myself a cup of tea to enjoy while I watched the sunset on my patio.

And something Callie told me seeped into my brain.

Word on the curb is that the cops arrested the wrong guy.

The feline is always telling me that cats know things. Plus, she's got an extensive network of animal sources across the island. Callie was instrumental in helping me discover the person who killed one of my former co-workers, a rival reporter at the *Palmchat Gazette*. I don't think I should ignore what she tells me, so I won't. I have to find out what, if anything, Willie Peters knows about Cynthia's murder.

"Sophia!" barks Marty.

Snapping to attention, I say, "Well, you see ... I can't really tell you why I don't think Willie killed Cynthia. I just ... don't."

Leaning over his desk, Marty scowls at me. "Well, Sophia, here's something I can tell you. If Willie Peters didn't kill Cynthia Snowpearce but he knows who did, then you better get that information. Or else ..."

An hour later, I'm back at the St. Mateo jail with a blank check in my purse and Marty's warning making me doubt my insistence on bailing Willie Peters out of jail.

I'm hoping against hope that Willie was being honest with me. And yet, as I stride into the building, I'm painfully aware that I took the word of a thief. Sure, Willie might not be a killer, but he could definitely be a liar. Maybe he only told me he had a big idea so I would bail him out. Maybe as soon as I bail him out, he'll have a sudden memory loss. Maybe he'll give me a fake name to some phantom person who doesn't exist.

Sighing, I groan.

Maybe I shouldn't have been so quick to—

"Sophie ..."

Startled slightly by the sound of my name, and at the same time recognizing the voice, I stop mid-stride, and pirouette to face Officer Noah Cuetee.

"What are you doing here?" asks Officer Cuetee as we move to the side of the wide hallway, out of the pedestrian traffic of police officers, attorneys, and concerned citizens.

"This will probably sound crazy," I begin. "But, I'm here to bail out William Peters."

Officer Cuetee frowns. "You want to bail out William Peters?"

Nodding, I say, "He says he didn't kill Cynthia Snowpearce—"

"Sophie, you do know that the jail is filled with people who didn't do it, right?"

Sheepish, I feel my cheeks warm when he gives me his teasing smile. "Yes, I know that, but ... as I said, this might sound crazy, but I think William Peters is telling the truth. And he's going to tell me who really killed Cynthia Snowpearce. But, first, I have to bail him out of jail."

Officer Cuetee shakes his head. "You can't do that."

"Why not?" I ask. "I have a blank check. My boss, Marty, is allowing me to draw the funds from the paper's petty cash account—"

"No, what I mean is," says Officer Cuetee. "You can't bail out William Peters because he's no longer in custody. He made bail last night ..."

Chapter 22

"So who bailed Willie Peters out of jail?" asks Callie.

The cat showed up ten minutes ago, a sight for sore eyes. I'd been feeling glum and sorry for myself, lying on the chaise lounge, consoling myself with a cup of lavender and blood orange tea as I'd watched the sun sink into the horizon.

"You won't believe this," I say. "Willie Peters."

Perched on the end of the chaise, inches from my crossed ankles, she stares at me. "I don't understand."

"Neither do I," I admit, biting my lower lip before telling the cat what Officer Cuetee told me. Despite the fact that Willie Peters claimed not to have any money for bail, he somehow came up with the cash and informed the court late yesterday afternoon.

"Somebody gave Willie the money," says the cat, licking her right front paw.

I take another sip of tea. "But who?"

"Somebody who wanted to stay anonymous," says the cat. "Otherwise, the person would have come to the jail to bail Willie out themselves."

"You're right," I say, sitting up and swinging my legs over, and placing my bare feet on the warm outdoor tile. "But again, who?"

"Who bailed him out doesn't matter," says the cat. "He's out. And it doesn't change the fact that he's got information you need, especially since that hamster is nowhere to be found."

"No luck in locating him, huh?"

"Girl, I told you I didn't think I would find him," says Callie. "I still think he's dead, but maybe not. After all, stranger things have happened."

Staring at the cat—who actually speaks to me—I can't help but giggle.

"What's funny?" demands Callie.

Waving my hand, I say, "Nothing. But, again, you're right. Willie Peters was supposed to tell me who killed Cynthia Snowpearce but that's not going to happen now."

"Who says it's not?" asks the cat, staring at me.

"Oh, well, um ..." I clear my throat. "I just thought, you know ... why would Willie Peters tell me anything? I didn't bail him out."

"But you were going to," says the cat.

"But I didn't," I remind her.

"Your intent matters," says the feline. "The way I see it, you were going to uphold your end of the deal. Willie Peters backed out on you. Technically, he owes you the name of Cynthia Snowpearce's killer."

Tilting my head, I stare at the cat. "Um, I'm not sure that Willie Peters will see it that way."

"Well, sis, you're going to have to make him see it that way," says Callie.

Confused, I ask, "How?"

"You still have the money you were going to use to bail him out?"

"I still have the blank check," I say. "I have to give it back to Marty, which I plan to do tomorrow. I couldn't bring myself to go back to the office and tell him that I didn't get the information he told me to get, or else."

"You can still get the information," Callie says. "You'll just have to pay Willie Peters for it."

"I don't know if Marty would want me to pay for the information," I say.

"The name of Cynthia Snowpearce's real killer is worth it," says Callie. "Think of it, sis. Your article could crack the case. You'll go viral and trend all over the internet. You'll get booked on all of those silly morning shows you humans like to watch when you should be getting the kids ready for school."

"You're right," I say, considering the cat's argument. "The killer's identity will be money well spent."

"You know Willie Peter's address?"

"I can look it up on the public records database app," I say.

Chapter 23

Nearly an hour later, I'm standing in front of Willie Peter's apartment.

The sun went down thirty minutes ago, and along with the indigo, star-filled sky came excitement and the feeling of embarking on a risky, breath-taking adventure. Driving to the location with that sassy, sarcastic cat in the passenger's seat, I felt a thrill of exhilaration. My dreams of becoming an award-winning investigative journalist felt as though they'd been reignited. I felt reinvigorated. Maybe even a little restored. I saw myself on Good Morning America. Good Morning Britain. I saw a new byline beneath my name. Sophie Carter, Investigative Reporter. I imagined having my own dedicated tip line, where hundreds of tipsters would call and leave messages, imploring me to investigate and uncover rampant corruption and crime.

All my desires, hopes, and wishes would come to pass because I would have cracked the Cynthia Snowpearce murder case. And Marty would be proud of me, and so happy to have such a young, tenacious, enterprising reporter on his team.

"Sophie Carter has 'it,'" he would tell *The New York Times*, *The*

Washington Post, and a whole host of other important publications that would call him for quotes about my sleuthing skills.

Unfortunately, however, none of my desires, hopes, and wishes will come to fruition if I don't get a chance to question Willie Peters.

That is, I won't crack Cynthia Snowpearce's murder if Willie Peters won't open the door, which I've been knocking on for the past minute, or two. Maybe three.

Lowering my hand to massage my sore knuckles, I glance down at Callie, standing near my right foot.

"Maybe he's not home," I say, trying not to feel deflated.

"Hmmm ..." purrs the cat. "Maybe. Maybe not. You stay here and keep knocking. I'll be right back."

"Where are you going?"

"To have a word with that lazy canine over by that tree ..."

"What?" I ask as Callie trots away, heading across the grassy quad in the center of the complex. About thirty feet away is a large coconut palm. Beneath it lounges a large St. Bernard. Curious and fascinated, I abandon my knocking to observe Callie.

The cat approaches the dog slowly, her steps cautious as she circles his huge, languid form. From my view, the dog appears to be asleep, but I'm not sure. Callie makes another circle around the dog, then inches closer to his head.

What is she doing? I wonder, biting my lower lip. The dog is ten times her size. He could easily crush her with his massive paw. Should I be worried? Does that sassy, sarcastic cat know what she's doing? And why does she want to have a word with the dog? About what?

Callie lifts her left paw.

I frown. What is she—

With lighting speed, Callie slaps the St. Bernard twice across its large nose.

Gasping, certain the St. Bernard will rip the feisty feline apart, I jog a few steps away from the door, not sure how I'm going to rescue the crazy cat, but—

The dog shakes its massive head then rises on all fours and backs away from Callie.

Shocked, I freeze in place as Callie raises her paw again, boxing it toward the St. Bernard. The big dog shakes his head again, then lowers it. What is happening? Is she fussing at the dog? Is the dog allowing her to berate him? I'm not really sure. I don't understand animal behavior. I never had pets when I was growing up. Okay, well, I take that back. I had a fish. I named him Tommy. Wait, no, Timmy. Or, was it … never mind, that doesn't matter. What matters is this conversation, if I can call it that, Callie and the St. Bernard seem to be having. Callie is hissing. The dog is barking. This back-and-forth barking, and hissing goes on for about a minute, then Callie turns from the dog and runs back toward me.

"What just happened?" I ask, lowering down to one knee when Callie stops near my foot.

"Willie Peters is inside his apartment," says the cat.

"How do you know that?"

"Bernie told me," says Callie.

"Bernie?"

"That lazy dog …" Callie turns her head in the direction of the coconut palm.

I glance toward the tree. Bernie the St. Bernard leans against the trunk, his tail sweeping the dirt encircling the palm.

"You know him?"

"We know of each other," clarifies Callie. "He's a canine of a canine."

"A canine of a canine?"

"What you humans call a friend of a friend," says Callie. "He's friends with Dutiful, Officer Dreamboat's Belgian Malinois."

"Oh …" I stand to my feet, intrigued by these odd animal

friendships and connections. "So, Bernie told you Willie Peters is in his apartment."

"Willie Peters hasn't left his apartment since he bailed out of jail," says Callie. "Bernie says there's a key under the welcome mat. He says that's what Peters used to open the door."

I glance down at the welcome mat, which is not very welcoming. It's a stained, matted rectangle of threadbare carpet that looks as though it should be contaminated.

"Get the key so we can open the door and go inside," instructs the cat.

"Wait," I tell her. "We can't just go into Willie Peters' apartment."

"We won't be breaking in," says the cat. "We have a key."

"But we don't have permission to use that key," I say. "Willie Peters could call the cops and have us arrested for—"

"Girl, why do you keep forgetting that I'm not catching a charge for you?" asks the cat, staring up at me. "And furthermore, sis, don't you want to crack the case and film a segment for Good Morning Caribbean?"

Biting my lip, I shake my head. "I feel like I'm going to regret this, but ..."

"But ...?"

'But sometimes, I ask myself, what would Vivian Thomas do?" I say, feeling a bit wistful. "She's my mentor and my idol. She's an award-winning investigative journalist who—"

"Girl, you could have gotten the key, opened the door, got the information from Willie, and left by now," says the cat. "Focus, sis. We can talk about your mentor later. I'll bet you she wouldn't hesitate to go inside Willie Peters' apartment."

"No, she probably wouldn't," I say, with more resolve and courage than I feel as I crouch down and lift the corner of the welcome mat with the very tips of my thumb and index finger—which I make a mental note to thoroughly disinfect as soon as possible.

Key in hand, I insert it into the lock, turn the knob, and push the door open.

The lights are off in the apartment, but it's not completely dark. A small lamp on an end table next to the couch, which is positioned against the left wall, offers a cozy glow. It's enough to guide me toward the light switch. With full illumination, I glance around the small space. The furnishings are sparse, but the place is tidy. And empty.

"I thought the St. Bernard said Willie Peters was home," I whisper, debating whether, or not, to make like a tree and leave. I want to be as brave as I know Vivian would be, but I have a sudden acute case of the willies—no pun intended. I'm seriously worried that Willie Peters is going to appear, possibly with some type of weapon, and he's going to attack me. After all, the key notwithstanding, I am in his apartment without his permission. He didn't invite me in, which means—

"What's that smell?" asks Callie.

I sniff the air, and frown. "Rancid goat milk?" I ask, remembering Mr. Beauchamp's description of Willie's malodorous presence.

"The other smell ..." says the cat, trotting away from me, disappearing around the corner of an entryway between the living room and another section of the apartment, most likely the bedroom or bathroom.

"What other smell?" I ask, following her down a short hallway, at the end of which is a half-opened door leading into a room.

"Callie, come back here ..." I whisper. "We need to leave ..."

One day, I will be as brave and fearless as Vivian Thomas, but today is not that day. The idea that Willie Peters is somewhere in the apartment waiting to pounce gives me the heebie-jeebies. Entering his apartment was a bad idea. I never should have let that crazy cat talk me into—

"We need to call the cops, sis ..." says Callie, poking her head around the door.

"What?" I rush toward her, my heart pounding.

Seconds later, in the bedroom, I realize why she wants to call the police.

A man lies face up on the bed, his unfocused, lifeless eyes staring toward the ceiling.

Gasping in shock, I inch toward the bed.

It's Willie Peters. Dead. With a purple and neon green tie wound tightly around his neck.

Chapter 24

"Girl, don't just stand there with your mouth hanging open," says the cat. "Call the cops."

"Yes, right, okay …" With trembling fingers, I delve my hand into my crossbody, pull out my phone, then turn and—

A masked figure stands a few feet away, blocking the door.

I scream.

The figure lunges at me.

Screaming in shock and surprise, I drop my phone and shuffle backward.

"Please, leave me alone!" I yell, continuing to walk backward as the figure advances toward me. "Don't hurt me, please don't—"

My calves bang against something hard, and as I lose my balance and fall backward, I realize it was the footboard of the bed. I land on a lumpy mass. Willie Peters, I think. Horrified, I flip over, trying to get away from the dead body, but I find myself face to face with Peters' pale gray face, staring into his dead brown eyes.

Scrambling, I flip away from Peters' dead body, this time catapulting myself onto the floor. Banging my shoulder against the wood floor, I groan.

"Sis, you okay ..."

Blinking my eyes, I glance at Callie.

"You didn't hit your head, did you?" asks the cat, placing her paw between my eyebrows. "You're not going to go into a coma again, are you?"

"No, no ..." I assure the cat as I push up onto my elbow. "I mean, I don't think so ..."

"Good," says the cat. "Because I have a plan."

"A plan?"

"To get us out of here alive," says Callie. "You distract the guy ... and then I'll go psycho cat on him."

Remembering how Callie went psycho cat on me, I say, "That'll work ..."

I jump to my feet.

The masked figure is on the opposite site of the bed.

"Listen ..." I start. "You don't have to hurt me. As far as I'm concerned, you were never even here. I mean, it's not like I could even identify you, or—"

The masked figure steps up onto the bed, advancing toward me.

"Wait ... " I take a few steps back. "Don't ..."

"Sis ... you're supposed to be distracting him!" I hear Callie say.

Not taking my eyes off the masked figure, I say, "I know that!"

"So distract him!"

"That's what I don't know..."

"Girl, if you don't—"

"Okay, okay ... um ..." Before I realize what I'm doing, I twirl around in a circle to the left ... and then I twirl around in a circle to the right ... then I tap my left foot in and out ... then I tap my right foot in and out ...

The masked figure stops and tilts his head to the right.

I tap my right foot to the front two times and do a cha-cha-cha. Then I tap my left foot to the back and do a cha-cha cha. Clapping my hands twice, I shimmy and side-shuffle right. Then I do a body roll. I clap twice again, shimmy, and side-shuffle left.

The masked figure tilts his head to the left.

I do a left shoulder roll and a shimmy, then a right shoulder roll and a shimmy, then I—

"Girl, what are you doing?" demands the cat.

"I'm distracting him ..." I say, doing a little body roll before I slide to the left.

"How? By doing the Palmchat Shuffle?"

"You have a better idea?" I ask the cat as the masked intruder stalks across the bed.

"Maybe try twerking," suggests the cat.

Frowning, I glance at her. "Well, I would, but I'm not that good at—"

"Forget it, sis," says the cat. "I got this!"

Seconds later, Callie leaps up onto the bed table and then lunges at the masked intruder like a wild cat, claws extended like Wolverine as she clamps onto the masked intruder's head. Having both witnessed and experienced the cat's savage psycho mode, I know the masked intruder is about to go down.

And that's why I'm stunned speechless when the masked intruder grabs Callie around her throat and yanks her away from his head.

"*Sacre bleu!*" says the masked intruder before he throws the cat away from him.

Gasping, my palm against my mouth, I follow the feisty feline's trajectory as she sails through the air, wailing in terror, and then hits the wall opposite the bed with a sickening thud.

"Callie!" I scream as the cat's body drops to the floor.

Without thinking, I dash over to the feline and drop to my knees next to her.

"Callie!" I lift the cat, praying nothing is broken, and carefully cradle her in my arms. "Oh, Callie! Talk to me! Please! Are you okay?"

Eyes closed, the cat doesn't respond.

"Callie, please! Open your eyes and speak to me!"

The cat remains prone, unmoving.

Fear and panic explode within me. Callie can't be dead! She just has to be okay. If the masked intruder killed her, then—

The masked intruder.

A new fear assails me.

I'm so worried about Callie's safety that I forgot about him.

Glancing over my shoulder, I'm praying he's not right behind me, ready to—

The masked intruder is gone.

Confused, I make my way to my feet. On wobbly legs, I glance around the bedroom. There's no one here except me, Callie, and poor Willie Peters. I hurry to the bed and sit on the edge.

"Callie, wake up," I tell the cat, blinking back the tears threatening to stream down my face. "Please, you have to. I mean, like, I think you really do have to wake up. You have nine lives, remember. As far as I know, you've only used one. Maybe two. Which means you have at least seven lives left!"

The cat doesn't respond.

"Oh, Callie, you can't die," I say, no longer trying to hold in my tears. "What will I do without you? You can't leave me. I still want to be your human. And I still want you to be not my cat. And—"

"Why you crying, sis?"

Shocked, I sniff and stare at Callie.

Her green eyes are open and focused on me.

"Callie ... " I whisper.

The cat places a paw against my wet cheek. "Calm down, girl. I'm not dead yet. And, by the way, I still have all nine lives left."

Overjoyed, I hug the cat tightly against me, even though she protests with hisses and growls, and kiss the top of her head several times.

"Sis, please!" Mumbles the cat.

After a few more hugs and kisses, I relax my hold.

"Girl, miss me with all that excessive affection," grumbles the cat even as she snuggles against me.

"Oh, Callie, I'm so glad you're okay," I tell her.

"Well, I'll be better if you tell me that the jerk who flung me against the wall like I was some flea-ridden alley cat was arrested," says Callie.

Sighing, I say, "Unfortunately, he got away."

"Figures," says Callie. "My surprise sneak attack wasn't a surprise or sneaky. He definitely saw me coming. He was ready for me."

"I'm afraid that was my fault," I confess. "Sorry I didn't do a good job of distracting him."

"Girl, I knew that Palmchat Shuffle wasn't going to work," Callie says. "You should have twerked."

Chapter 25

"Do the cops have any suspects?" Asks Clark, taking a sip of his coffee.

"None that they're sharing with me," I tell Clark, and then take a sip of vanilla rose tea.

Sitting at a table near the windows in the breakroom, Clark and I are enjoying a respite from what has been, thus far, a rather slow news day.

Several days have passed since Callie and I discovered Willie Peters' dead body in his bedroom. After Callie regained consciousness, I called the police. Twenty minutes later, Officer Cuetee, his partner, and two other deputies showed up.

While the other cops secured the crime scene, Officer Cuetee guided me into the living room.

"Are you okay?" asked Officer Cuetee.

With a shaky breath, I told him, "Yeah, I'll be fine."

"What were you doing here?"

"I came to interview Willie Peters," I said, and then went on to explain to Officer Cuetee why I wanted to talk to Willie, and I came clean about how I got into the apartment.

"How'd you know about the key under the welcome mat?"

Gently rocking Callie, I said, "Oh, Bernie told Callie, and—"

"Bernie told Callie?" Officer Cuetee frowned. "Who is Bernie? And ... do you mean Callie your cat?"

Once again, I mentally kicked myself. "Oh, um ... Callie is not my cat, remember? And, you know ... people keep spare keys under the mat, so I just thought ... you know."

Officer Cuetee gave me an odd look that held hints of suspicion and amusement. He was about to ask me another question, but the crime scene techs showed up, followed by Detective François, who demanded to question me.

"The person who killed Willie Peters has to be the guy who attacked you," says Clark.

"That's what I think," I say, running a finger around the rim of my teacup. "But who was that guy? I couldn't even give the police a good description. He was wearing a mask."

"Did he say anything to you?" asks Clark.

I shake my head. "I don't think so. Not that I can remember."

"Well, I guess we know now that Willie Peters was telling the truth," says Clark. "He didn't kill Cynthia Snowpearce."

"I think the guy who killed Willie killed Cynthia, too," I say, recalling the garish tie cinched around Willie's neck. "It was the same manner of death. Strangulation by tie."

"Well, maybe the crime scene guys can get DNA from the tie," says Clark. "Otherwise, I'm not sure how the killer will be identified."

After draining my teacup, I say, "I might already know the killer's identity if ..."

"If ..." prompts Clark.

I clear my throat, thankful I caught myself before telling Clark that I would know the identity of the killer if Callie and I had talked to the hamster before he disappeared. Instead, I say, "If ... I had been able to bail Willie Peters out of jail. Then he would have shared that information with me."

"And you don't know who bailed him out?"

"Willie Peters bailed himself out, remember?"

"I mean, who gave him the money," says Clark. "He told you he was broke."

"I don't know," I say. "Maybe some Good Samaritan."

Frowning, Clark says, "I doubt that."

"You're probably right," I agree, contemplating another cup of tea. "But now that we're talking about this, I wonder ..."

"What?"

"Well, Willie was willing to trade the identity of Cynthia's killer for his freedom," I say. "What else would he be willing to trade for his freedom?"

"I'm not sure I follow you."

"Honestly, I'm not sure I follow me, either," I say. "But, when I talked to Willie, he seemed willing to promise anyone anything to get out of jail."

"So, maybe he promised someone else something else to secure his freedom," says Clark. "Okay, but what else could he trade his freedom for? You think someone else wanted to know who killed Cynthia?"

"I'm not sure," I say, biting my lower lip. "I guess it depends on who bailed him out."

"Which we don't know," says Clark. "But maybe we could find out."

"How?"

"Maybe we could talk to his lawyer ..."

Thirty minutes later, Clark and I are in my cubicle, using my desk phone to converse with Willie Peters' lawyer, Bradford Taylor, who we have on speaker so we can both hear him.

"Sad news, but not surprising," says the lawyer, whose gruff, gravelly baritone sounds as though it belongs to an overweight man who regularly smokes cigars. "Most of these crooks can't be helped. They end up in jail or dead. One or the other was bound to happen to Willie. My money was on life in prison, but I lost that bet. Willie ended up in the dirt. Rest his felonious soul."

I glance at Clark, who's giving me a look akin to the way I feel, which is that the lawyer's judgment of Willie is both shady and heartfelt.

Clearing my throat, I say, "Mr. Taylor, we don't want to take up too much of your time—"

"No worries!" assures the lawyer. "I spend so much time talking to unrepentant, irresponsible criminals that it's nice to converse with people who haven't broken the law."

"Okay, well," I begin, "do you happen to know who bailed Willie Peters out of jail? I mean, I know he bailed himself out, but when I spoke to him, he indicated he was indigent, so ... "

"How did he get the bail money?" The lawyer lets forth a booming chuckle. "Beats me! Your guess is as good as mine."

"What is your guess?" asks Clark.

"Well, if I had to guess, I probably wouldn't," says the lawyer. "After all, what does it matter? Willie's dead. But, I can tell you this ... the money came from an anonymous person."

"An anonymous person?" I echo.

"The cash was left on the doorstep of my office," says the attorney. "It was in an envelope with an anonymous note instructing me to give the money to Willie for his bail, and so I did. I wasn't there when the envelope was left, so I didn't see the person."

Disappointed, I sigh and slump back in my swivel chair.

Clark asks, "You have any idea who killed Willie Peters?"

"If I had to bet money on it, and perhaps I would, depending on the odds, of course," says the attorney, "I would say that Willie got himself killed on account of those diamonds he helped Cynthia Snowpearce steal ... "

Chapter 26

"There hasn't been much movement on the case," says Officer Cuetee.

Currently, on this glorious day in paradise, we're at the dog park, where he asked me to meet him after I called him this morning for an update on the Willie Peters murder case.

"The crime scene guys are testing the murder weapon, the silk tie, for sweat DNA," continues Officer Cuetee.

I stare at him. "Sweat DNA?"

Officer Cuetee explains that, in some instances, human sweat can be used as evidence to identify a person.

"But, there'll only be sweat DNA if the killer wore the tie before he killed Willie Peters."

"Willie and Cynthia were both killed with brightly colored ties," I say. "And I think those ties belonged to Willie. He told me that Cynthia bought the ties for him. I doubt the crime scene guys will find the killer's sweat DNA."

"If Willie was killed with his own tie, then I suppose it might be unlikely that the killer's DNA is on the tie," says Officer Cuetee. "Then again, I suppose the killer could have had sweaty palms."

Considering his point, I nod. "That's true. Strangling someone has to be very labor intensive. A macabre form of exercise when you think about it."

"And people get sweaty exercising," says Officer Cuetee.

"Does François think that Willie and Cynthia were killed by the same person?"

Officer Cuetee sighs. "I'm not sure."

"Does he think Willie was killed because of the diamonds he and Cynthia stole from Beauchamp's jewelry store?"

"François is, of course, not saying much," says Officer Cuetee. "Sorry I don't have much to tell you."

"No, it's okay," I say. "I expect Detective François to remain silent. Tell me what you think."

Officer Cuetee looks at me. "I think that Willie might have been killed by a fence, or maybe there was a third partner. Someone who didn't want to share the diamonds."

I say, "You know that makes me wonder ..."

"Wonder what?"

"Was Willie killed because he wouldn't hand over the diamonds? Or, maybe because he didn't know where they were, but the third partner didn't believe him?"

"Or, maybe the third partner did get the diamonds from Willie," opines Officer Cuetee. "But he killed Willie anyway, to get rid of loose ends. With both Cynthia and Willie out of the way, the third partner would not have to worry about splitting the money three ways."

Taking a deep breath, I glance at the dogs frolicking and running around in the fenced enclosure. "That's true, but—"

"Hey, is that the cat that's not really your cat ..."

"What?"

"She doesn't look so good," says Officer Cuetee.

"Huh ...?" I stare at Officer Cuetee.

Tilting his head, Officer Cuetee points at something to my left.

I turn my head in that direction.

The Calico is several feet away, walking across the grass toward me. My heart drops into my stomach. The feline is limping, definitely favoring her left hind leg.

"Callie!" I jump up and hurry toward her. Dropping to one knee in the grass, I reach forward and scratch behind her ear. "Are you okay? Does your leg hurt? It's not broken, is it?"

"Sis, please ..." The cat bobs away from my hand, then sits in the grass. "My leg is fine. It's not broken."

"Are you sure?" I ask. "You were, if you recall, thrown against the wall like a flea-ridden alley cat."

"Girl, don't remind me," says the cat, licking her fur. "Anyway, I came to tell you that the hamster is alive."

"The hamster is alive?" I'm flabbergasted, which is an understatement. "Wait. What? How? Where is he?"

The cat answers my questions: "Yes. The hamster is alive. I don't know. I don't know."

"This is great news!" I say. "Although, I wish we knew where he was."

"I'm working on it, sis," promises the cat.

Maneuvering into a sitting position, I stare at the cat. "Tell me why you're limping. Does your leg hurt? Be honest."

The cat gives me a look. "Okay, even though it is not any of your concern, if you must know—"

"Yes, I must know," I tell her, crossing my arms over my chest.

"My leg is a little sore," admits the cat. "But—"

"Oh, Callie, I knew you were in pain!" I roll over and stand on my knees. "I knew that terrible, horrible, no good, very bad masked intruder had hurt you!"

"Calm down, sis," says the cat.

"Calm down?" I gape at the feline. "How can I calm down when you're hurt? Oh, Callie, you need to go to the—"

"Forget it, sis," says the cat, pushing herself to all fours. "I am not going to the—"

"—vet," I say. "You have to, Callie."

"Girl, I said no," says the cat, backing away from me. "I am not going to the vet!"

"But, Callie, you need to find out if your leg is broken, or—"

"I'm not going to end up like Blanca!" hisses the cat.

"I'll make sure nothing bad happens to you," I say, reaching for Callie.

Hissing, Callie swats my hand, then turns and runs off, but not as fast as she usually does. There's a clearly discernable limp, giving her a lopsided gait that worries me …

"Sophie …"

Taking a deep breath, I get to my feet and turn.

His handsome face concerned, Officer Cuetee asks, "Everything okay?"

"Unfortunately no," I tell him. "Everything is not okay."

Chapter 27

Around nine in the morning, when I should be fact-checking articles instead of checking my social media feeds, my desk phone buzzes.

Startled, I peek at the Caller-ID.

My heart sinks.

It's bad news.

In other words, it's my boss, Marty. Why is he calling? To chew me out about my last few articles. According to him, they weren't great but not as terrible as he expected them to be.

Sighing, I put off the inevitable and press the speaker button. "Good morn—"

"Sophia. In my office. Now."

"Oh. Okay. Yes. Absolutely," I say. "I'll be right ..."

The line goes dead.

" ... there," I mumble, grabbing a yellow legal pad and a pen.

Ten minutes later, I'm sitting in the chair in front of Marty's desk. My boss paces behind his desk, smashing his stress ball between his palms.

"I need you to do a follow-up with Ephraim Beauchamp," barks Marty.

"Ephraim Beauchamp," I recite as I write the name on my legal pad. "Follow up story."

"Now that the cops know who stole his diamonds," says Marty. "I want you to find out if they've given him any information about the location of the jewels."

"I doubt he knows anything," I say.

Marty stops pacing to scowl at me. "And why do you doubt it?"

"Because I think the location of the diamonds is a secret that died with both Cynthia and Willie," I say. "And the more I think about it, I think the killer has the diamonds."

"The guy who attacked you," says Marty.

Nodding, I say, "I believe he took the diamonds from Willie and then strangled him to death."

"You're lucky he didn't strangle you," says Marty.

I stare at my boss. Wait. Is that ... concern in his gaze? Nah. Can't be. Must be some weird trick of the overhead fluorescent lights. Anyway ...

Clearing my throat, I say, "He did much worse to Callie."

"Callie?" Marty frowns. "You talking about that feral cat who put you in a coma?"

"Callie is not feral," I tell him.

"But she did put you in a coma."

"Well, yes, technically, she did," I concede. "But, she's since apologized. She didn't mean to go psycho on me. She doesn't really know why she attacked me because according to her, she's a *sophisticat*, not an alley cat, so—"

"Wait. Wait. Wait." Marty growls, stopping me. "What are you talking about?"

I blink. Wait. What was I talking about? Oh my goodness. Was I saying too much? Was I talking about the cat like she's my friend and not my cat? Wait. She's not my cat. What I meant was—

"What do you mean, the cat apologized?" demands Marty. "And she doesn't know why she attacked you? How do you know that?"

"Oh. Um. Well. You see ..." I clear my throat and jump up. "You know, I should probably go and call Mr. Beauchamp now before his store officially opens."

Pivoting, I nearly stumble and fall in my haste to get out of Marty's office.

Back at my desk, I dial the number for Beauchamp & Daughters. The line rings four times before Mr. Beauchamp picks up. "Good morning! You have reached Beauchamp & Daughters fine jewelry! It is my pleasure to serve you so please tell me how I may do so!"

Buoyed by the effusive greeting, I say, "Good morning, Mr. Beauchamp! It's Sophie Carter from the *Palmchat Gazette*! How are you this morning!"

"Oh, Ms. Sophie Carter from the *Palmchat Gazette*!" sings out Mr. Beauchamp. "I am doing wonderful on this delightful morning! And how are you?"

"I'm doing great," I tell him. "I was wondering if you have a moment to chat before your store opens. I just have a few questions."

"Yes, Ms. Sophie, I have time," says Mr. Beauchamp. "What do you want to ask me?"

"Well, it's about your stolen diamonds," I began. "Now that the police have identified the culprits—"

"*Zut alors!*" exclaims the diamond store owner. "I normally do not like to speak ill of the dead but I am glad those awful people got what they deserved!"

Not surprised by his sentiment, I ask, "Do the police have any leads about where your diamonds might be?"

"Alas, *non!*" He says. "They claim they are still on the case, but I do not think they care. They expect me to just write off the diamonds and collect the insurance money, but I cannot."

"Why not?" I ask.

"Because, *zut alors*, the diamonds were not insured for the amount they were worth."

"They weren't?" I ask, shocked.

"They should have been, of course," says Mr. Beauchamp. "But insurance is so very expensive. Many small jewelers like myself are forced to underinsure our gems. Those diamonds were worth two million dollars but I only insured them for two hundred thousand!"

"Oh no, Mr. Beauchamp," I say, sorry for his predicament.

"I fear the gems have been fenced and are long gone," he laments. "*Sacre bleu!* It is depressing and disheartening, but this horrible ordeal has taught me one thing."

"What's that?" I ask.

"I must get a better surveillance system," says Mr. Beauchamp. "My daughters have been telling me for years to upgrade my security and they were right. Anyway, Ms. Sophie, I am sorry but I must go. I have to finish the preparations for the opening of the store."

"Oh, of course, Mr. Beauchamp," I say. "And thank you for talking to me."

After I hang up the phone, I jot down notes from the conversation for my follow-up article, and then decide to head to the breakroom for a cup of tea. Opening the bottom drawer of the file cabinet next to my desk, I select a box of coconut and passionfruit tea.

As I leave my cubicle, something Mr. Beauchamp said floats into my mind, giving me a disturbing and strange feeling for some reason.

Sacre bleu!

Where have I heard that phrase before?

Chapter 28

"You found the hamster!"

Stunned, I stare at the cat as several emotions swirl and whip through me.

Sprawled on the lounge on my patio, the Calico licks her left foot. I'm sitting on the balcony railing, drinking a mug of tea, and trying to regain my balance. I almost fell off after Callie announced her breaking news. Fifteen minutes ago, I was getting ready to enjoy the sunset after a long and uneventful news day when I spied the feline approaching my patio. She walked slowly, and her gait seemed off. She seemed to be making an effort not to limp but I could tell she was favoring her injured leg.

Following greetings, she found her favorite place on the lounge, but she didn't leap up onto the cushions like she normally does. Instead, she carefully used her front paws to hoist herself onto the chair. I had to stop myself from helping her, knowing how independent she is. And I bit my tongue and didn't bring up visiting the vet to check out her leg, knowing she would refuse.

"Where has he been?"

"Girl, it's a wild story," says Callie, "in more ways than one."

"What do you mean?" I ask.

"After he was let loose in the jungle," begins Callie, "he came across a group of wild hamsters who took him in, fed him, and promised to protect him."

"Wow," I say. "So where is he now?"

"Girl, living in the jungle with his wild cousins," says the cat. "Word is, he loves it. Believes he was born to be wild and can't see himself being a house hamster ever again."

"Interesting," I say. "So … did he tell you who killed Cynthia Snowpearce."

"I didn't actually talk to him," says Callie. "That gossipy bird told me. So I told her to tell the hamster that I need to talk to him. He's going to meet us at the Valley of Waterfalls this Saturday so clear your schedule, sis."

Saturday didn't come soon enough, but the big day is here now.

My excitement is off the chart.

I can't wait to talk to the hamster, even though I won't really be talking to him. Callie will be translating, but the point is, I will finally find out who killed Cynthia Snowpearce. Which is the same person who killed Willie Peters before attacking me.

I can already see the story trending on the *Palmchat Gazette* website. I can see myself doing segments on Good Morning Caribbean, Good Morning Britain, and Good Morning America. I can see my new byline—Sophie Carter, Senior Investigative Reporter.

"Ready to go, sis?" asks Callie, sitting in the passenger seat next to me.

Starting the JEEP, I nod. "I am so beyond ready."

The weather is great. Warm and sunny. One of those picture-perfect paradise days that tourists travel to the island to enjoy. I'm looking forward to a long winding drive along the coast and into the jungle interior. Before leaving, I packed a tote bag of snacks. Treats for myself and tuna—fresh, of course—for Callie. Plenty of water for both of us.

"You know, I've never been to the Valley of Waterfalls," I say, pulling out of the resident parking lot behind my apartment complex.

"Well, I hope you know how to get there," says Callie, licking her fur. "I am not in the mood to get lost."

Chuckling, I say, "Don't worry. I have GPS on my phone. Have you ever been?"

"I've been a few times," says Callie. "With the tomcat."

After checking to make sure the road is clear, I turn out of the complex. "You know, I don't remember asking, but did you tell me the tomcat's name?"

"Thom Katt," says Callie.

I glance at the feline. "Thom Katt. The tomcat's name is ... Thom Katt?"

Callie stares at me. "Is there some kind of problem with his name?"

"No, no ..." I stifle a giggle. "Just sort of ... ironic. Anyway, how are things going with you and Thom Katt?"

"Well, things were going great until ..."

"Until ... what?" I ask, my springy curls blowing in the sea-scented wind as I follow the GPS's disembodied instructions.

"Until an issue came up."

"What sort of issue?" I ask, and then say, "And yes, I know it's not my business, but I must know."

The cat licks her fur and makes a purring sound. "The issue is Ginny ..."

"Who's Ginny?" I ask, navigating a traffic circle.

"This silly little Ginger cat," says Callie. "Ginny is the tomcat's ex."

"Oh, I get it," I say. "Ginny wants the tomcat back."

"Girl, it's worse than that," says Callie. "Ginny just had a litter of kittens. Seven of them. And she's claiming that the tomcat is the father."

"Are you serious?" I ask, riveted by this piping hot tea.

"As serious as a long-tailed cat in a room full of rocking chairs," says Callie.

"Well …" I say as I take the entrance onto the coastal road. "Is Thom Katt the father?"

"He claims he isn't."

"You believe him?"

"I don't know," confesses the cat. "But, I hope he's not."

"Do you want a family?" I ask, taking a quick glance at the cat.

Staring at me, she says, "I don't know. I mean … what if I already have a family?"

"You mean … what if you already have kittens?"

"Well, if I do, I don't remember them," says Callie. "Thanks to this selective catnesia."

"Speaking of the selective catnesia—"

"Let's not," says the cat.

"Not only could a vet tell if you're microchipped, but he could determine if you've given birth," I say. "And he could take a look at your leg."

"Girl, I told you my leg is fine."

"You're still limping," I tell her, though when she showed up on my doorstep this morning, her limp was less pronounced. Nevertheless, I'd hate to think that her leg was fractured and healed improperly.

Saying nothing, the cat licks her fur.

"Look, I thought you wanted help with the selective catnesia."

"I do," says Callie. "But can't you help me without forcing me to see a vet?"

"Actually," I say, recalling the CCTV cameras across from the *Palmchat Gazette* building. "I may have a way to do that. But I need to check out some things first ..."

Chapter 29

Guided by the GPS and various road signs, Callie and I arrive at our destination.

According to the St. Mateo guidebook, the Valley of Waterfalls is one of the main island attractions, with annual visitors in the hundreds of thousands. After finding a space in a gravel parking lot near a souvenir shop, the cat and I grab a complimentary map of the area from a nearby kiosk.

"Where are we meeting the hamster?" I ask, opening the map, which features dozens of hiking trails.

"Follow me," says Callie.

We head along a gravel path through dense trees. The jungle air is humid and balmy, fragrant with the smell of flowers and lush vegetation. As I marvel at the various species of flora and fauna, I reach into my cross-body for a scrunchie and use it to pull my curls into a ponytail.

Fifteen minutes, and way too many meandering twists and turns along too many trails and pathways crowded with tourists, later, the cat and I make a detour, descending through the rainforest. Callie tells me we're meeting the hamster, and his four jungle cousins, beneath a tree in the backyard of an empty luxury cabin along the river.

Moments later, sitting on a bench carved from a palm tree, I watch as Callie circles the hamsters, who scurry and growl.

The most obvious difference between Cynthia Snowpearce's pet hamster and the wild hamster cousins is their color. The traumatized pet hamster is golden, but the cousins have black bellies with golden and white faces.

"What's happening?" I ask, hoping the feline won't scare the hamsters.

"Relax, sis," says the cat. "The cousins are just making sure that the hamster wants to talk to us willingly. Witnessing the violent murder of his owner was very traumatic for the hamster and the cousins don't want him to have to relive any horrible memories if he doesn't have to."

"Oh, of course not," I say. "Please tell the cousins that I will not push the hamster to relive any terrible memories."

"Girl, please," says the cat, staring at me. "We didn't come all the way out here for nothing. He's going to talk to us, or else."

Squeaking and squawking, the cousins close ranks around the hamster.

"What's happening?" I ask the cat.

"The cousins are warning me not to threaten them," says the cat before she raises a paw toward the jungle hamsters. "That wasn't a threat, Jimmy, that was a promise."

"Callie!" I admonish. "Do not antagonize the cousins!"

"Girl, I'm not scared of them," says the feisty feline. "At the end of the day, they're just rats."

One of the hamsters scurries toward Callie, chittering loudly.

"I said what I said, Jimmy," says the cat.

I pinch the bridge of my nose. "Please don't vex them."

The cat hisses at the hamsters, then says, "Look, Jimmy, we don't want any smoke, okay?"

"We want no smoke whatsoever, Jimmy," I say. "None at all."

Callie turns her head to look at me. "Girl, he can't understand what you're saying, you know that, right?"

"Well, tell him," I implore. "And tell Cynthia's hamster that I don't need gory details. Just the name of the person who killed his owner."

The cat focuses on the hamsters. "Jimmy, is he ready to talk, or what? Because we do not have all day."

Jimmy scurries back to the cousins and the golden hamster. There's a bit of squeaking and some growling from the other three wild cousins. Worried, I bite my lip. I'm so close to finding out who killed Cynthia Snowpearce. So close to being able to crack a huge murder case. So close to proving to Marty that I am a good investigative reporter and I do have 'it.' If the cousins renege on their promise to allow Cynthia's hamster to tell me his story, then I don't know what—

The golden hamster scurries forward.

Relief floods me.

A hushed silence seems to descend over the atmosphere as he begins his eyewitness account, which sounds to me like a series of squeaking chirps.

"What is he saying?" I ask the cat, after a minute or two.

Callie says, "It was a dark and stormy night once upon a time in a galaxy far, far away …"

Tilting my head, I say, "Are you serious?"

"Girl, this hamster is, as you humans would say, a ham," says Callie with a hiss. "He's got a captive audience and he plans to do the absolute most … "

Shrugging, I activate the recording app on my phone.

The hamster scurries from side to side, squeaking and chirping up a storm.

Callie translates: "Cynthia was getting ready for bed ... she'd just fed the ham and he was prepared to call it a night, as well ... and then all of a sudden, there was banging at the front door ... so, Cynthia put on her robe and left the bedroom to go and see who was at the door ... the ham wondered who it could be, but figured it was Cynthia's boyfriend, Willie, who sometimes came over late at night and ..."

"And ..." I prompt, as Callie trails off

The cat hisses at the golden hamster. "Keep it clean, okay? Nobody is interested in your R-rated version of events!"

I stifle a giggle.

The golden hamster continues.

Callie says, "But it wasn't Willie at the door ... it was a man ... he and Cynthia started arguing. The man wanted to know where his diamonds were ... "

"Where his diamonds were," I whisper, intrigued as the hamster continues to squeak and chirp.

"Cynthia said she had them but she was not going to give him the diamonds," translates the feline. "She told him that he would have to pay her for the diamonds. The man offered Cynthia ten thousand dollars, but she wanted more because she knew the jewels were worth two million dollars ... "

"Two million dollars," I echo, finding the sum frighteningly familiar.

"The man said he would give her fifty thousand," says Callie, translating the hamster's chirps. "Cynthia refused. She wanted two hundred thousand dollars. The man said that was out of the question. Cynthia said he would never see the diamonds and she would find someone to fence them for her. Cynthia told the man to show himself out and she returned to the bedroom. But the man didn't show himself out ..."

"What did he do?" I ask, even though I already know.

The golden hamster ceases his chirping.

Jimmy and the other cousins growl at Callie and then huddle around the golden hamster.

"What's happening?" I ask.

"He needs a moment," says Callie. "And I could use some sustenance. Where's that tuna?"

"I think I left it in the JEEP," I say.

"Girl, are you serious?"

"I'm sorry, but ... how can you eat at a time like this?"

"Girl, it's intermission," says the cat. "That's when you humans get snacks and wine, right?"

"Callie, this is not a Broadway show," I scold, disappointed at her lack of compassion.

"Girl, you could have fooled me," says the feline. "This is better than a Lifetime movie."

Exhaling, I shake my head.

The golden hamster begins squeaking again.

Callie says, "The man came into the bedroom. Cynthia screamed at him to leave. But the man grabbed Cynthia and slapped her. Then he punched her. Cynthia fell to the floor."

"Oh no," I gasp, my hands flying to my mouth.

The golden hamster chirps.

Callie says, "Then the man grabbed a tie that was on the dresser ... Cynthia was going to give it to Willie as she always bought him ties ... she always wanted Willie to dress like a gentleman and not like a bum, but it was no use because he was a bum ... anyway, the man wound the tie around Cynthia's throat ... "

"Oh, my God!" I say.

"The man choked her with the tie until he killed her," says Callie.

"The hamster says he is devastated because there was nothing he could do … he was unable to escape his cage … if he could have, he would have gone for the man's beady little eyes … "

Stunned and shaken, I ask Callie, "Does he know the killer's name?"

"You know who killed her?" Callie asks the hamster.

The golden hamster growls for a full minute.

Callie says, "He says that after the man killed Cynthia, his cell phone rang. The man had the audacity to answer the call … it was as though he hadn't just murdered a woman in cold blood … and when the man answered the phone, he said, *'this is Ephraim Beauchamp'*."

Chapter 30

Still reeling from the hamster's shocking revelation, I take a sip of lemon tea and stare at Callie.

Hours have passed since we returned to my apartment.

As I drove from the Valley of Waterfalls, the cat and I discussed the stunning developments. Ephraim Beauchamp killed Cynthia Snowpearce and Willie Peters. To say I'm shocked would be an understatement. And yet, I wonder if I should be shocked. After all, I suppose there were lots of clues that led to Mr. Beauchamp as the killer. Unfortunately, I didn't pick up on those clues. Which makes me wonder if Marty is right about me. Maybe I'm not a good investigative reporter. Maybe I don't have it. Maybe I'll never be a senior reporter. Maybe I won't write articles that trend and—

"Okay, sis, now what?" asks Callie, licking her fur.

I glance at the cat. "I'm not quite sure."

"What do you mean, you're not quite sure?" demands the cat. "You know who killed Cynthia Snowpearce. You have to write the story that cracks the case. You have to tell the cops."

"What if the police don't believe me?"

The feline turns her head to lick her neck. "Why wouldn't they believe you?"

"Because I have no proof," I say, taking another sip of tea.

"You have the hamster's eyewitness account," counters the cat.

"Callie, do you hear yourself? A hamster's eyewitness account?" I scoff, shaking my head. "The cops aren't going to take me seriously. They are going to think I'm crazy."

"Well, you're probably right," agrees the cat. "So, how are you going to get proof that Ephraim Beauchamp is a murderer?"

"I'll have to trick him into confessing," I say.

"Easier said than done," says the cat.

"True, but …" I take another sip of tea. "Now that we're talking about this, I'm thinking there might be a way to trick Mr. Beauchamp …"

"And what's the way?" asks Callie.

"Well, Mr. Beauchamp killed Cynthia Snowpearce because she stole his diamonds but refused to give them back when he refused to pay her the money she wanted for them," I say. "And I'll bet Willie was killed for the same reason. Mr. Beauchamp needs those diamonds. They're worth two million dollars. But he can't collect the insurance money because he had to underinsure them because the insurance was too expensive."

"He can't afford to write off that big of a loss," says Callie.

"No, he can't," I say. "He might have to declare bankruptcy. Or be forced to close his business."

"You know that makes me wonder something," says Callie. "Obviously Beauchamp knew that Cynthia Snowpearce and Willie had robbed him. Why didn't he tell the cops?"

"Why did he go to Cynthia and offer her money for the diamonds?" I ask.

"Girl, something is fishy about this story and it's not that tuna you gave me."

I drum my nails against the table. "Here's what I'm thinking …"

"Why don't I like the sound of that?" asks Callie.

"A sting operation."

"Have you forgotten what happened the last time you tried to pull off a sting?"

"This time, it's going to work," I promise her. "Beauchamp wants those diamonds. I'm going to give them to him."

"But you don't have the diamonds."

"Beauchamp doesn't know that," I say. "I'm going to tell him that I have his diamonds and I'll give them to him … if he tells me the truth about what happened to Cynthia Snowpearce and Willie Peters. And, unbeknownst to him, I'll be secretly recording him. And then I'll use the recorded admission of Mr. Beauchamp's guilt to write my story before I give it to the police so they can arrest him and put him behind bars where he belongs."

The cat stares at me. "Girl, you think it's going to be that easy?"

"I know it's going to be risky, but—"

"But you really think Beauchamp is going to admit that he murdered two people?"

"He is desperate for those diamonds," I tell Callie.

"Yeah, that's the problem," says the cat. "He's desperate enough to kill for those diamonds."

"Don't worry, okay," I say. "I am going to insist that we meet in a public place so he can't wrap a tie around my neck and strangle the life out of me."

"I still don't like this sting operation idea," says Callie, stretching out on the table.

"Well, I don't like that you refuse to go to the vet about your leg," I counter.

"Don't deflect," warns the feline.

Jumping up from the table, I grab my cell phone, then return to my seat. Following a quick sip, or three, of tea for courage and tenacity, I dial Mr. Beauchamp's number.

It rings a few times, and then he answers with a curt, "What?"

"Beauchamp?" I say, disguising my voice, using a lower pitch so that, hopefully, I sound like a grizzled old longshoreman, down on his luck, looking for work on the marina.

"Who is this?"

"I have your diamonds," I say.

"My diamonds?"

"The gems Cynthia and Willie took from you."

After a pause, Beauchamp says, "Where are they?"

"If you want them, then I want $1,000.00 ..."

"A thousand dollars?" Callie jumps to all fours. "Girl, you better ask for more than that. And I thought you were supposed to ask him to tell you the truth about what happened to Cynthia and Willie."

Lowering the cell phone, I whisper to the cat, "I'm going to demand that when I meet with him in person. I'm going to do a bait and switch."

"Bait and switch?" asks Callie.

"I'm going to offer him a better deal," I say. "The truth for the diamonds, which will actually save him money."

The cat tilts her head. "And what if he would rather pay you?"

"Well—"

"Hello?" says Beauchamp, his voice loud enough to hear even though I'm holding the phone away from my ear. "Are you still there?"

"Yes, yes ..." I say. "Sorry about that. Um, as I was saying, if you want the diamonds, I will need—"

"A hundred thousand," says Callie.

"A hundred thousand." I frown. "He might not agree to give us that much."

"He wants those diamonds, doesn't he?"

"Well, yes, but we need to agree on an amount in order for the sting to work, so—"

"Hello? Are you still there?"

"Oh, yes, of course, Mr. Beauchamp, I'm still here ... "

"Girl, disguise your voice," chastens Callie.

Praying Beauchamp didn't catch my slip, I say, in the disguised voice, "Um, I mean, yes, I am still here ... and I want ... ten thousand dollars ... "

"I thought you said you would give me the diamonds in exchange for a thousand dollars," says Beauchamp.

"Did I ...?"

"Yes, you did," insists Beauchamp.

"Oh, well ... " I clear my throat. "I was mistaken. I meant to say—"

"Twenty-five thousand," says Callie.

"Twenty-five thousand," I echo, glancing at the cat.

"Wait just a minute," says Beauchamp. "You said ten thousand for the diamonds!"

"My apologies," I say. "I was, again, mistaken. I meant to say twenty-five thousand."

"This is extortion!" shouts Beauchamp. "Highway robbery!"

"Actually," I say, "it's a steal."

"I beg your pardon!"

"Well, I was going to ask you for a hundred thousand," I tell him. "You're getting a seventy-five percent discount."

"Hmmm ..." murmurs Beauchamp. "When you put it that way..."

"Do we have a deal?" I ask, crossing my fingers and my toes.

"D'accord," says Beauchamp. "When and where will we meet to make the exchange?"

"Um, how about we meet at ... "

"The dog park," says Callie. "If he tries any funny stuff, I'll sic those canines on him."

"The St. Mateo dog park," I tell Beauchamp. "At two o'clock tomorrow."

"*D'accord*," says Beauchamp. "I will see you then. I will have the cash. Make sure you have the diamonds."

When I end the call, Callie says, "Girl, we could have gotten more than that from him ..."

Chapter 31

"This does tastes wonderful!" I gush, taking another sip of the tea, a delightful new flavor I've never had before but which Officer Cuetee discovered while on a break during his shift, and which he found so tasty, that he just had to buy a box for me to try.

He showed up at my apartment twenty minutes ago, after sending a text asking if I was free and didn't mind a visitor. Of course, I told him to come over. Officer Cuetee works a lot of double shifts, so it's always a delight when he can make time to see me. I was alone and didn't mind company since Callie had skedaddled a few hours ago.

"I thought you would think so," he says, smiling as he savors another sip. "Unfortunately, I haven't found a good donut hole pairing. Maybe you could help me with that."

"Mint, cucumber, and coconut," I say, taking another sip. "It tastes so refreshing ..."

Nodding, Officer Cuetee says, "Maybe something with lime."

"This tea deserves something crisp and clean," I say.

"That's a good way to describe the taste," says Officer Cuetee, placing his empty mug on the table. "Clean."

At once, something about the word 'clean' gives me a spasm of guilt.

Before Callie left to visit Thom Katt, the tomcat, she advised me to tell Officer Cuetee about the plans for my sting operation, but I just shrugged and told her I would think about telling him. Of course, I don't want to get him involved. He's going to advise me against the sting operation. Tell me it's too risky. Too dangerous. After all, I'll be dealing with a cold-blooded murderer. A man who's killed two people.

But, now I'm thinking maybe the cat is right.

"What do you think about that?" asks Officer Cuetee.

I glance at him. "What do I think about what?"

His aqua-blue eyes grow concerned. "Hey, are you okay? All of a sudden, you seem ... "

"Guilty?" I say, propping an elbow on the table.

Across from me, Officer Cuetee frowns. "I was going to say pensive. But now I have to wonder ... is there something you feel guilty about?"

"Okay, I need to come clean," I say, and then confess my plan to trick Mr. Beauchamp into confessing that he committed double homicide.

"Let me guess," says Officer Cuetee, folding his arms across his chest. "You were feeling guilty because you weren't going to tell me about this plan because you know I'm going to tell you that it's too dangerous and I don't want you to do it."

Sighing, I say, "Well ... yeah."

"Sophie—"

"I know it's a dangerous plan, but—"

"If Ephraim Beauchamp really did murder two people, then—"

"No, he's totally the killer," I insist.

"You have proof of this?"

"Well, um ..." I bite my bottom lip, recalling what the hamster told me and Callie. "Sort of, but ... not exactly."

"Sort of but not exactly?" Officer Cuetee scowls in a way that makes him look even cuter, if that's possible, which obviously it is because, well, he looks even cuter.

I say, "There was a witness to Cynthia Snowpearce's murder."

"Who is the witness?" demands Officer Cuetee.

"The witness wishes to remain anonymous," I say. "But the witness saw Mr. Beauchamp killed Cynthia Snowpearce because Cynthia stole his diamonds."

"You spoke to this anonymous witness?"

Nodding, I say, "Yes ... well, I didn't speak to him myself. His story was translated to me because ..."

"Because?" prompts Officer Cuetee.

I clear my throat. "The anonymous witness doesn't speak ... English. Anyway, Mr. Beauchamp knew that Cynthia Snowpearce and Willie Peters robbed his store. And Mr. Beauchamp went to Cynthia Snowpearce to get his diamonds back, but she wanted two hundred thousand dollars, which he didn't have, so he killed her."

"And he took the stolen diamonds?"

I shake my head. "I think Mr. Beauchamp looked for the diamonds in Cynthia's house, but he couldn't find them. So, he went to see Willie Peters. I think Willie might have demanded more money than Mr. Beauchamp wanted to pay. And I'll bet the anonymous person who paid for Willie's bail was Mr. Beauchamp."

Officer Cuetee rubs his jaw. "You might be right."

"I think it makes sense," I say. "Mr. Beauchamp agreed to bail Willie out on the pretense that he was going to pay Willie for the diamonds, but that was a lie."

"Maybe Beauchamp and Willie went back to Willie's place," says Officer Cuetee. "Instead of paying Willie, Beauchamp demands that Willie give him the diamonds."

"Of course, Willie refuses," I say. "So, he killed Willie. Then, Beauchamp decided to search Willie's place for the diamonds, but I showed up and interrupted him."

Stroking his jaw, Officer Cuetee says, "Okay, if you're right about Beauchamp, and I have a feeling you might be, then you need to tell Detective François everything you've told me."

Groaning, I say, "I knew you were going to say that."

"Sophie, I know you want to do the sting operation so you can get your exclusive story—"

"Exactly," I agree. "I have to prove to Marty that I have 'it', that I deserve to be a senior investigative reporter, that I've shaped up so he doesn't have to ship me out."

"You won't be able to write that exclusive story if you're dead," says Officer Cuetee. "If Beauchamp killed Cynthia Snowpearce and Willie Peters, then he's beyond dangerous. He's homicidal."

Slouching in my chair, I roll my eyes. "Yeah, that's what Callie said ..."

"Callie?" asks Officer Cuetee, confusion in his tone. "Are you talking about Callie the cat who's not your cat? That Callie?"

Sitting up, I clear my throat, and say, "You know, you're right. I should let Detective François handle things. After all, he's one of the famous François brothers. If anyone can get Beauchamp to confess, Detective François can. We should call him right now, don't you think?"

Giving me a slightly suspicious look, Officer Cuetee says, "I have his number in my contacts. I'll send him a quick text."

I nod as Officer Cuetee rises from the table and strides to the breakfast bar where he placed his phone.

Letting out a long, low sigh, I resist the urge to smack my forehead. When am I going to remember that I can't talk about Callie as though she's a friend and not a cat I know? I can't imagine what Officer Cuetee thinks. I probably seem like a crazy cat lady. One of those people who think they can communicate with their felines. But the weird thing is, I *can* talk to the Calico.

My cell phone chirps, signaling a text.

Distracted, I grab it and check the message.

I have your cat.

"Okay …" Officer Cuetee returns to the table. "I sent Detective François a text."

Frowning, I text back, *I don't have a cat.*

"He texted me back," says Officer Cuetee. "He's in St. Xavier right now, but he will meet with us tomorrow morning. How about that?"

Nodding, I say, "Yeah, that's—"

My cell phone chirps again.

"Hold on a sec," I tell Officer Cuetee. "I think someone has the wrong number. I need to tell them …"

The message on my phone is a photo that sends my heart into my throat.

Gasping, I whisper, "Oh no …"

"What is it?" Officer Cuetee asks.

Words fail me as I stare at the picture.

It's Callie … locked in a small cat carrier.

"Sophie …"

Struggling to breathe, I say, "Callie has been … catnapped!"

Chapter 32

My phone chirps again, a horrible, traumatizing sound.

Officer Cuetee grabs my cell phone and reads the text message. *"If you want your cat back alive, come to 8099 Seagrass Circle …"*

"Oh my God … " I wail. "Oh, poor Callie!"

"Looks like the number is anonymous so I can't trace it," says Officer Cuetee. "You recognize the address?"

I shake my head. "No, I don't …"

"That's okay," says Officer Cuetee, standing. "Come on …"

Shell-shocked, I stare up at him. "Huh?"

"We're going to go get that cat you know that's not your cat."

Swallowing my fear, I nod and rise to my feet.

Thirty minutes later, Officer Cuetee steers his police-issued cruiser alongside the curb of the address I was texted to come to if I want Callie back alive, which of course I do.

The threatening text has been swirling around in my head, like a horrible curse. *If you want your cat back alive.* Meaning, if I didn't show up at the address, then Callie will be—

I perish the thought.

I can't bring myself to think the worse.

More than anything, I want the sassy, sarcastic, feisty, fierce cat to be okay.

I want all nine of her lives to be safe and sound.

Officer Cuetee shifts the car into park. "Okay ... let's find out who lives here."

As he uses an index finger to look up the address on the touch screen of the computer table mounted to his dashboard, I stare through the passenger window at the house. It's a large, sprawling bungalow in an upscale part of the island known for its large, sprawling bungalows. Someone in this beautiful house has Callie. But who? What fiendish, heartless catnapper owns this place? And why did they catnap Callie?

At once, something occurs to me.

The catnapper didn't give me a ransom demand. The text just said if I want to see Callie alive, I was to come to this address. The person would not have catnapped Callie if they didn't want something in return. So, what could they possibly want from me? I have no idea. All I know is that, so far, I've held up my end of the bargain. I'm here at this house, as requested, so Callie better still be alive, or—

"Odd ..." mumbles Officer Cuetee.

I turn to look at him, focusing on his silhouette in the darkened interior. "What's odd?"

"You'll never guess who this house belongs to," says Officer Cuetee.

"Normally, I like guessing games, even though I'm not super good at them, but I'm not really in the mood to guess, so please just tell me—"

"Ephraim Beauchamp."

Gasping, I gape at Officer Cuetee. "What? Wait. Are you serious? That homicidal diamond-obsessed psycho has Callie? Oh my God! We have to rescue her!"

Horrified at the thought of Callie in the clutches of that murderer Beauchamp, I grab the inside door handle, and—

"Sophie, wait!" Officer Cuetee places a hand on my forearm, stopping me.

"I can't wait!" I tell him. "I have to get Callie away from that psycho killer!"

"That's why you have to wait," says Officer Cuetee. "If Beauchamp is a killer, then he won't hesitate to hurt you, and I'm not going to let anything bad happen to you, okay?"

Blinking back tears, I say, "I just don't want him to hurt Callie."

"That's why you need me to check out things first," says Officer Cuetee. "Obviously, Beauchamp took Callie to lure you here."

"But why would he do that?"

"I'm guessing he knows you're behind the sting operation," says Officer Cuetee.

"That's not possible," I say. "I disguised my ..."

"You disguised ... what?"

"I was going to say my voice," I say, a sinking feeling settling into the pit of my stomach. "And I did disguise my voice except for one time when I forgot."

"That one time might have been enough for Beauchamp to recognize your voice," says Officer Cuetee.

"You're probably right," I say, sinking into the seat. "And because of my stupid mistake, Callie got catnapped by a homicidal maniac, and if anything happens to her—"

"Hey, don't worry," says Officer Cuetee, slipping an arm around me. "I won't let anything happen to the cat who's not really your cat."

Smiling through my tears at him, I whisper, "You promise?"

"You promise to stay in the car and let me handle things?"

Nodding, I say, "Okay ... "

Twenty minutes later, I'm still in the police cruiser waiting.

Twenty minutes ago, after exiting the vehicle, Office Cuetee walked up the long circular driveway to the wide porch. He took the stairs two at a time and strode to the double doors. Watching, I was able to see him ring the doorbell. A few seconds passed, and then the door opened. There was some conversation between Officer Cuetee and whoever had opened the door—Beauchamp, I assumed—and then he entered the house.

The doors closed and my blood pressure spiked.

It's still through the roof.

Shouldn't Officer Cuetee have gotten Callie and returned to the car by now? I'm trying not to think the worst, but how can I not? Beauchamp didn't catnap Callie just to hand her over to the cops. If Beauchamp recognized my voice, then obviously, he took Callie because he wants to trade her for the diamonds.

Sighing, I wring my hands, wishing I had a strand of pearls to clutch, which is ironic considering that Mr. Beauchamp tried to sell me a strand of pearls.

Callie was right.

The cat told me that the sting operation wasn't a good idea. I should have listened. Instead, I was too caught up in writing an explosive, exclusive story. I ignored the danger and downplayed the risks because I wanted to prove that I have 'it' and that I should be a senior investigative reporter.

I fight tears. Callie just has to be okay. I can't stand the thought of her in the carrying cage. She's such an independent feline. Being cooped up probably sent her into psycho cat mode. Try as I might, and even though I know Officer Cuetee will make sure Callie is okay, I can't stop worrying. Mr. Beauchamp is a vicious murderer. If he hurts Callie—

My cell phone chirps.

Startled, with trembling fingers, I pull it from my cross body and stare at the message.

Cat is safe and Beauchamp in handcuffs.

Flooded with relief, I text back, *oh thank goodness!*

I'm going to call for backup. You can come get the cat. She wants to get out of the carrier.

on my way, I text.

Giddy with excitement and happiness, I jump out of the car and hurry to the door.

Chapter 33

Seconds later, I rush into the spacious foyer and hurry down a long wide hallway that opens into a large living area.

Abruptly, I stop.

Roughly fifteen feet ahead is Officer Cuetee.

But he's not handcuffing Mr. Beauchamp.

He's tied up like a wild Billy goat in one of two cane chairs separated by a round bamboo coffee table.

"Sophie!" Officer Cuetee cries out to me. "No! Don't—"

I run toward Officer Cuetee. "Oh my God, what happened?"

"Beauchamp got the jump on Officer Dreamboat ..."

Recognizing that sassy sarcasm, I turn in the direction of the voice.

Callie is trapped in a small cat carrier, which sits on a side table against a wall.

"Beauchamp tased me," says Officer Cuetee, his breaths coming in panting gasps. "Then he restrained me while I was incapacitated."

"Oh no ..." I walk over to Officer Cuetee. "Let me get you untied."

"Don't bother, sis," says Callie.

"You can't," says Officer Cuetee.

"Beauchamp used Officer Dreamboat's own handcuffs against him," says Callie.

"Beauchamp secured me with my own handcuffs," says Officer Cuetee, whose arms are positioned behind the back of the chair, his wrists secured with the cuffs, making it impossible for him to get free.

"Where's the key?" I ask.

Callie says, "Beauchamp took the keys."

"Beauchamp took them," says Officer Cuetee.

"Drats!" I say, biting my bottom lip.

"Girl what did I tell you about mentioning food?" asks the cat.

I turn to her. "I said 'drats', not 'rats'."

"Oh, I thought you said rats."

"No, I said drats," I tell the cat. "You know, it means like—"

"Sophie!" says Officer Cuetee.

Startled, I face him.

He frowns at me. "What are you talking about?"

"Oh. Um. Well. You see—"

"You need to get out of here," says Officer Cuetee. "Call the police. "

"Right," I say, shoving my hand into my cross body. "I will call the police …"

"Tell them to send backup," says Officer Cuetee.

Nodding, I make the call. Once I'm done, I face him, "The dispatcher said she's sending several officers right now."

"Okay, now you get out of here," says Officer Cuetee. "Go back to the car, and—"

"I can't leave you here alone with that crazy maniac," I dispute.

"Is he telling you to leave? Girl, you better listen to him!" says the cat. "You and I need to get out of here before Beauchamp comes back!"

"Where is Beauchamp?" I ask.

Officer Cuetee says, "I don't know … he got a call and then he went into another part of the house, but—"

"Oh no, that was Beauchamp who texted me," I say.

"What do you mean?" asks Officer Cuetee.

"I got a text from you saying that Beauchamp had been arrested," I say. "That's why I came into the house."

"Girl, Beauchamp tricked you!" says Callie.

"He must have lured you into the house to hurt you," says Officer Cuetee. "You've got to get out of here now!"

"Okay, okay, I'm going," I tell him.

"Come on, sis," says Callie. "Let's go!"

Hurrying to the cat, I say, "Oh, Callie!"

"Sophie what are you doing?" demands Officer Cuetee.

"I have to get the cat," I tell him.

"Don't worry about that cat," says Officer Cuetee.

"How can I not worry about Callie?" I demand.

"Girl, did he tell you not to worry about me? Don't listen to him," says Callie. "Worry about me! I've been trapped in this carrier for a dog's age and Beauchamp is treating me like a hostage! I haven't had any food or water in hours! I'm going to have a panic attack if I don't get out of here!"

"Sophie! Don't—"

"It'll take me just a second to get the cat," I tell Officer Cuetee.

Grabbing the cat carrier, I turn and—

Beauchamp stands a few feet away, pointing a gun at me.

Chapter 34

My heart sinks as my mouth goes dry.

"Ms. Sophie Carter of the *Palmchat Gazette*," says Beauchamp in his ebullient tone, though his smile is sinister. "It's so very good to see you."

Shaking my head, my body poised to flee, I step back. "Listen, I don't—"

Beauchamp's arm snakes out and his hand clamps around my wrist. Before I can scream, he shoves me to the floor. I hit the hardwood as the cat carrier drops to the floor with a fatalistic thud.

"Oh, sis, I'm getting a bad feeling!" wails Callie. "We have to get out of here before he kills all of us!"

"Get up!" commands Beauchamp, brandishing the weapon at me.

Trembling, I scramble to my hands and knees before staggering to my feet.

Beauchamp grabs my arm and shoves me toward the empty cane chair next to Officer Cuetee. Shrieking, I stumble into the chair, grabbing the armrests so I won't fall. Staring at Beauchamp, I try to take a deep breath but I'm finding it difficult to breathe at the moment.

"Sophie, just do as he says, okay," whispers Officer Cuetee. "Don't antagonize him. Everything's going to be okay. We're going to get out of here—"

"Shut up, you fool!" commands Beauchamp.

"Mr. Beauchamp …" I shake my head, staring at him. "Look, you can't kill me …"

"And why can't I?" demands Beauchamp, brandishing the gun at me. "Tell me, why shouldn't I do to you what I did to Cynthia Snowpearce and that dolt Willie Peters?"

"Because I can get you your diamonds," I say.

"Stop telling lies and making false promises!" Thunders Beauchamp. "You're just like Cynthia! She lied to me, too. Told me she would give me the diamonds if I gave her fifty thousand dollars. I agreed. Then she changes the price. Says she wants two hundred thousand or I'll never see the diamonds again! Wretched trollop!"

"So then you killed her?" asks Officer Cuetee.

"Not on purpose," says Beauchamp, his gun still trained on me. "I just wanted to scare her into telling me where the diamonds were, but she wouldn't …"

"It was probably hard for her to talk with a tie wrapped around her neck," I mumble.

"What did you say?" demands Beauchamp, sneering at me.

"Um …" I clear my throat. "I know you probably didn't want to hurt her … or Willie Peters."

Beauchamp barks a vicious laugh. "Oh, no, I meant to kill that idiot. He thought I was a fool. I agreed to bail him out of jail because he told me Cynthia had given him the diamonds to hide. We agreed on a price of twenty-five thousand dollars, enough cash for him to leave the island and avoid prosecution. I brought the money. And he tried to give me cubic zirconia! Fake diamonds. Did that fool think he could fool me? Did he think I would not know a fake stone when I saw one?"

"Mr. Beauchamp," I begin, hoping to appeal to whatever, if any, humanity remains within him, "I don't understand. I mean, you've killed two people over these diamonds when you could have just gone to the cops and told them you knew that Cynthia and Willie had robbed you."

"The police would have arrested them," says Officer Cuetee. "And the District Attorney could have offered them a deal for a lesser sentence if they agreed to return the diamonds to you."

"I couldn't go back to the police," says Beauchamp. "I took a risk reporting the diamonds stolen in the first place, but I needed to get those diamonds back. I was hoping the cops would locate the diamonds even though I knew that if they caught Cynthia with the jewels, she would have told them that I'm not just a diamond broker, but I also do some fencing myself."

"Are you serious?" I ask, shocked. "You're a diamond fence?"

Beauchamp rolls his eyes. "Oh, don't look so shocked. It's more of a side hustle than a full-time gig. I even fenced a few pieces for Cynthia which was why I could not believe it when she stole from me!"

"What is he saying?" asks Callie.

"So … you fenced jewelry for Cynthia and then she stole from you," I say, translating for Callie.

"Girl, I guess it's true what they say," says Callie. "No honor among thieves."

I'm about to agree with Callie, but I catch myself, remembering that I can't talk to the cat and other humans at the same time. Well, I mean, technically, I can. But, I shouldn't because it gets really complicated and hard to tell who I should respond to, and then—

"And she didn't just steal a few pieces that I could care less about," continues Beauchamp. "She stole diamonds that were already stolen!"

"Diamonds that were already stolen," says Officer Cuetee.

"What do you mean?" I ask.

"I fence for the island cartel," says Beauchamp. "Specifically, I fence the diamonds stolen by the cartel's diamond thieves."

"So Cynthia stole stolen cartel diamonds," I say.

"Diamonds I must get back," says Beauchamp. "Or the cartel will kill me!"

"Mr. Beauchamp, listen," I say, a plan forming, one that could set me free, or get me killed. "I really do know where the diamonds are ..."

Beauchamp gives me a shrewd look. "I don't believe you."

"It's true," I say. "When I interviewed Willie Peters, he told me where they were hidden."

Officer Cuetee asks, "Is that true?"

Continuing with my ruse, which I'm praying will work, I say, "He wanted someone to know where they were just in case something happened to him. He wanted the diamonds to be given to charity."

Beauchamp's eyes narrow. "You really know where Willie hid the diamonds?"

Nodding, I say, "I do ..."

"Where are they?" demands Beauchamp.

Despite my uncertainty about the location of the diamonds, I say, "You don't think I'm just going to tell you, do you?"

"You will if you don't want a bullet in your head," says Beauchamp. "Remember, I killed Cynthia and Willie. I'll kill you, too."

"And if you shoot me," I say, "you won't get the diamonds. You will never guess where they are. And the cartel will kill you."

Beauchamp rubs the barrel of the gun against his chin. "I suppose you're right."

"I am right," I say, trying to inject confidence in my tone. "So, if you want the diamonds, then you and I will have to go together and—"

"Tell him that he has to let me out of this carrier and then you'll take him to the diamonds," says Callie.

I glance at the carrier. "What?"

"What … what?" Beauchamp gives me a confused frown.

"Girl, just do it," says Callie. "I got a plan, too."

"No, I don't want him to hurt you," I say, not caring that I sound like I'm reciting non sequiturs for no reason.

"You don't want who to hurt who?" asks Officer Cuetee.

"I don't have time for this nonsense!" shouts Beauchamp. "You take me to get the diamonds, or I will—"

"Tell him to let me out of this carrier," says Callie.

"What is wrong with that stupid cat?" demands Beauchamp. "Why does it keep meowing, meowing, meow, meow, meow!"

"Girl, is that old geezer mocking me?" asks Callie. "What is he saying? I heard meow."

"If you want the cat to stop meowing, you'll have to let her out of that carrier," I say.

"Girl, that is not what I told you to tell him," says Callie.

Realizing my mistake, I say, "Um, actually, what I meant was … if you want me to take you to the diamonds, you'll have to let her out of that carrier."

"What?" Beauchamp and Officer Cuetee say this at the same time and give me pretty much the same look, which is one of confusion.

"You heard me," I tell Beauchamp. "If you want the diamonds, you have to let the cat out of the carrier."

"Are you serious?" asks Officer Cuetee.

Nodding, I say, "Absolutely!"

Beauchamp exhales. "*Zut alors! D'accord!* I will let the cat out, and after I do, you will take me to get the diamonds."

Worried that Callie's plan might be as foolish as my failed sting operation, I say, "Right. Absolutely. So, the sooner you let her out, the sooner we can go and get the diamonds."

"Sophie, what are you doing?" whispers Officer Cuetee.

"Actually, I'm not quite sure," I admit.

With the gun trained on me, Beauchamp crouches in front of the cat carrier. He uses his free hand to open the door. As soon as he does, Callie leaps onto his face, sinking her claws into his cheeks.

Roaring in pain, Beauchamp drops the gun and grabs Callie with both hands.

"Don't you ever throw me into a wall again!" says the cat, even though Beauchamp can't understand her.

"*Sacre bleu!*" wails Beauchamp as the feline hisses in his face.

Terrified that he'll throw her again, I jump up and lunge for the gun. Grabbing the firearm, I point it at Beauchamp. "Freeze! Don't move!"

At my command, Callie scampers down Beauchamp's body and trots over to Officer Cuetee.

"Now, turn around," I tell Beauchamp. "Slowly ..."

Expelling a string of curses, Beauchamp ignores me and instead takes off running.

"Shoot, girl!" says Callie.

"I don't know how to use a gun!" I admit.

"Girl, are you going to let him get away?" asks Callie.

The front door bursts open just as Beauchamp sprints into the foyer. A half dozen St. Mateo police officers crowd into the foyer. Beauchamp tries to turn and run, but the cops converge on him, dragging him to the floor as he thrashes and curses. In seconds, the police cuff him and read him his rights.

Dropping the gun, I run over to Officer Cuetee, and find Callie sitting on his lap, looking content and comfortable.

"Looks like she likes you," I say, reaching out to scratch the cat behind her left ear.

Shaking his head, Officer Cuetee chuckles. "Lucky me ..."

Purring, Callie says, "Don't mention this to the tomcat, sis."

Lifting Callie from Officer Cuetee's lap, I tell him, "Just need a moment with the cat that's not my cat."

"Where are you taking me?" demands Callie as I walk toward a corner, so Officer Cuetee can't hear us.

"If you want me to stay quiet," I say, glancing over my shoulder, relieved to see two deputies working to free Officer Cuetee. "Then you need to agree to do something for me."

"And what would that be?"

I give the cat my terms.

"Sis, that's blackmail," says Callie.

"Yeah," I say, kissing the top of her head. "It is ..."

Chapter 35

"I can't believe that Mr. Beauchamp killed Cynthia Snowpearce and Willie Peters," says Clark, taking a sip of coffee. "And he was a diamond fence."

"I agree," I say, taking a sip of tea. "Mr. Beauchamp was so charming and engaging. Who knew he was a crook and a murderer?"

Clark and I are enjoying early morning libations in the breakroom before the nine o'clock staff meeting with Marty.

"Well, I guess your anonymous eyewitness source knew," says Clark.

Nodding, I smile as I reflect on the hamster who cracked the case, now living in the wild, enjoying life in the jungle with his black-bellied cousins.

"But, actually," I say, remembering a conversation I had with Officer Cuetee a few days ago, "Mr. Beauchamp was on Detective François' suspect list. Apparently, Francois never really thought Willie Peters had killed Cynthia."

"Why did François suspect Beauchamp?" asks Clark, sipping more coffee.

"The sweat DNA found on the tie that was used to kill Cynthia came back as a positive match for Mr. Beauchamp," I say. "His DNA and fingerprints were in some Interpol database from crimes he committed a few years ago. He was the leader of a smash-and-grab gang in Aruba, which is sort of hard to believe."

"Is there any evidence that he killed Willie Peters?"

"Beauchamp's DNA was on the tie used to kill Peters," I say. "And his fingerprints were all over the apartment. Officer Cuetee says François thinks Beauchamp was searching for the diamonds when Callie and I showed up. After attacking us, Beauchamp had to get out of the apartment, so he didn't have time to clean up his prints."

"So, are you going to have to testify against him?" asks Clark.

I pop a donut hole into my mouth and shake my head. "I don't think so. Apparently, Detective François wants to force Beauchamp to flip on the island cartel, so Beauchamp might take a plea deal for a lesser sentence if he snitches."

Scoffing, Clark says, "You mean if he's alive long enough to snitch."

"Exactly," I say.

Glancing at his watch, Clark says, "Ten minutes until the meeting."

Groaning, I stand. "Don't remind me."

After Clark and I dispose of our trash, he says, "I almost forgot to ask you this: what about the stolen diamonds? Did the cops find them?"

As we leave the breakroom, I say, "As far as I know, the diamonds are still wherever Cynthia Snowpearce hid them."

Clark says, "In other words, nowhere to be found ..."

Epilogue

"Is Callie going to be okay?" I ask Dr. Amos, the vet at the St. Mateo Animal Clinic.

A week has passed since Callie grudgingly agree to see a vet about her injured leg. While we were still at Beauchamp's bungalow, I put her down for a moment to answer Detective François' questions and she ran off. She kept her distance for a while, which sent me into a worrying tizzy, but today, when I went out to my JEEP at lunchtime, she was sitting on the hood.

"Callie!" I cried out as I ran to her. "Where have you been? I have been worried sick!"

"Here and there, sis," said Callie, licking her fur. "You know me."

"Why did you disappear from Beauchamp's house?" I asked. "I was just getting ready to put up flyers all over the city."

The cat gave me a look. "Girl, you really do the most sometimes. Look, I'm back, so no need to worry anymore. And ..."

"And?" I'd crossed my arms.

"And I'm sorry for worrying you," apologized the cat. "I was mad that you blackmailed me into going to the vet and then I realized, you can't talk to the tomcat. The two of you wouldn't understand each other, so technically, you can't blackmail me."

Tilting my head, I said, "Guess you're right about that."

"And you are right about the vet," said the feisty feline. "Girl, my leg has been killing me. I have to see what's wrong with it."

And so, Callie and I headed to the animal clinic.

While we waited, Callie fretted, complaining about how long it was taking to see the vet, lamenting that she might catch fleas from some of the other animals, and worrying that she'd end up like her friend Blanca who went into the animal clinic but never came out.

Twenty minutes later, Callie went into the examination room, where I sat on a stool in the corner while the doctor checked her out. Afterward, a nurse took her to another room to get a shot to prevent fleas. I was prepared to go with her, but the doctor wanted to speak with me, and Callie told me she could handle the nurse.

"If she tries any funny business," said Callie as the nurse scooped her up, "I'll scratch her eyes right out of her head."

Holding my breath, I stare at Dr. Amos.

"She's going to be fine," says the vet. "Her leg is not broken."

"Thank God!" I say.

"But, it is sprained," Dr. Amos tells me.

"Oh no," I lament.

"Parts of the ligaments are torn," he says. "And she does have some swelling, for which I'm going to prescribe a non-steroidal anti-inflammatory medication. This will help speed healing and recovery and reduce pain."

"Thank you," I say.

"With plenty of rest, Callie will be back on her feet in no time," says Dr. Amos, as he scrawls across a prescription pad.

Clearing my throat, I ask, "Doctor, before we go, would it be possible for you to do one more thing?"

"What's that?"

"Can you see if Callie is microchipped?"

"So, what's the prognosis, sis?" asks Callie, lounging in the passenger seat of my JEEP as I back out of the parking space in the animal clinic lot. "Will I live?"

"None of your nine lives are in jeopardy," I say, biting my lip, worry and panic slithering through me.

"Is my leg going to fall off?"

I force a laugh despite my dour, pensive mood. "No, silly ... it's just sprained. You need plenty of rest. You can't be walking on that leg. And I'm going to have your prescription filled."

"Prescription?" The cat asks. "I have to take medicine?"

"It'll help with the swelling and the pain," I say, gripping the steering wheel with damp palms as I pull out onto the main road.

"Okay, sis, what are you not telling me?"

I give Callie a quick glance before focusing on the road again. "What do you mean?"

"There is something you are not telling me," says the cat.

"Why do you think there's something I'm not telling you," I say, trying to keep my voice airy and innocent.

"Because cats know things," she says. "I can tell you are keeping something from me and I want to know what it is!"

Exhaling, I press my foot against the brake as the traffic light turns red. "Okay, okay ..."

"Spill it," demands Callie.

"I asked the vet to see if you're microchipped," I confess, pressing the gas after the light turns green.

"You what?" demands the feline.

"And you are," I say, feeling as glum as I sound.

"I am?"

Nodding, I say, "You have a microchip."

Callie asks, "And what does that mean?"

Blinking back tears, I say, "It means ... I know who your real owner is ... "

Can't get enough of Sophie and Callie?

Check out their next mystery in A Foul and Frightening Tail.

A celebrity target. A criminal pack. The only way to catch these perps is to go off leash...

A Foul and Frightening Tail is the delightful third book in the high-spirited Sassy Sarcastic Cat Cozy Mysteries. If you like sun-kissed beaches, light-hearted humor, and companions with serious cattitude, then you'll love Rachel Woods' purrfect page-turner.

Buy A Foul and Frightening Tail to pounce on the truth today!

Hey, y'all, hey!!!

Subscribe to my newsletter and you'll get inspiring rescue stories, hilarious cat memes, and thrilling serialized fiction. Plus, you can find out first about new books featuring my fabulous life as a feisty, fierce feline, and much more!

Sign me up!

Sassy Callie

https://subscribepage.io/SassyCallie

Also by Rachel Woods

SASSY SARCASTIC CAT COZY MYSTERIES

Sophie Carter, a struggling reporter for the *Palmchat Gazette,* teams up with a sassy talking Calico cat to solve crimes as she strives to become an influential investigative reporter

A SLY AND SINISTER TAIL

A COLD AND CALCULATING TAIL

A FOUL AND FRIGHTENING TAIL

REPORTER ROLAND BEAN COZY MYSTERIES

Roland "Beanie" Bean, husband and loving father, finds himself the unwitting participant in solving crimes as he seeks to make a name for himself as a reporter for the *Palmchat Gazette.*

HAPPY BIRTHDAY MURDER

EASTER EGG HUNT MURDER

MERRY CHRISTMAS MURDER

TRICK OR TREAT MURDER

GOBBLE GOBBLE MURDER

HAPPY 4TH OF JULY MURDER

SUMMER VACATION MURDER

PALMCHAT ISLANDS MYSTERIES

Married journalists, Vivian and Leo, manage the island newspaper while solving crimes as they chase leads for their next story.

UNTIL DEATH DO US PART

NO ONE WILL FIND YOU

YOU WILL DIE FOR THIS

DON'T MAKE ME HURT YOU

THE PALMCHAT ISLANDS MYSTERIES BOX SET: BOOKS 1 - 4

RUTHLESS REVENGE ROMANCE SERIES

Gripping romantic suspense series with steamy romance, unpredictable plot twists and devastating consequences of deceit.

HER DEADLY MISTAKE

HER DEADLY DECEPTION

HER DEADLY THREAT

HER DEADLY BETRAYAL

MURDER IN PARADISE SERIES

A series of stand-alone women sleuth mysteries with murder, mayhem and a dash of romance, set against the backdrop of turquoise waters and swaying palm trees of the fictional Palmchat Islands.

THE UNWORTHY WIFE

THE SILENT ENEMY

THE PERFECT LIAR

About the Author

Rachel Woods studied journalism and graduated from the University of Houston where she published articles in the Daily Cougar. She is a legal assistant by day and a freelance writer and blogger with a penchant for melodrama by night. Many of her stories take place on the islands, which she has visited around the world. Rachel resides in Houston, Texas with her three sock monkeys.

For more information:
www.therachelwoods.com
rachel@therachelwoods.com

facebook.com/therachelwoodsauthor
instagram.com/therachelwoodsauthor
bookbub.com/authors/rachel-woods
amazon.com/author/therachelwoods

About the Publisher

BonzaiMoon Books is a family-run, artisanal publishing company created in the summer of 2014. We publish works of fiction in various genres. Our passion and focus is working with authors who write the books you want to read, and giving those authors the opportunity to have more direct input in the publishing of their work.

For more information:
www.bonzaimoonbooks.com
info@bonzaimoonbooks.com

facebook.com/BonzaiMoonBooks
twitter.com/bonzaimoon

Made in the USA
Middletown, DE
12 July 2023

35007157R00106